As a child, **Anna Cleary** loved reading so much that during the midnight hours she was forced to read with a torch under the bedcovers, to lull the suspicions of her sleep-obsessed parents. From an early age she dreamed of writing her own books. She saw herself in a stone cottage by the sea, wearing a velvet smoking jacket and sipping sherry, like Somerset Maugham.

In real life she became a school teacher, where her greatest pleasure was teaching children to write beautiful stories.

A little while ago, she and one of her friends made a pact to each write the first chapter of a romance novel in their holidays. From writing her very first line Anna was hooked, and she gave up teaching to become a full-time writer. She now lives in Queensland with a deeply sensitive and intelligent cat. She prefers champagne to sherry, and loves music, books, four-legged people, trees, movies and restaurants.

THE ITALIAN
NEXT DOOR…

BY
ANNA CLEARY

First published in Great Britain 2011
by Mills & Boon, an imprint of Harlequin (UK) Limited,
Eton House, 18-24 Paradise Road, Richmond, Surrey TW9 1SR

© Ann Cleary 2011

ISBN: 978 0 263 22082 7

Harlequin (UK) policy is to use papers that are natural, renewable and recyclable products and made from wood grown in sustainable forests. The logging and manufacturing process conform to the legal environmental regulations of the country of origin.

Printed and bound in Great Britain
by CPI Antony Rowe, Chippenham, Wiltshire

*For Bess, Jan and Liz,
three of the dearest sisters on the planet.*

*Also, I extend the most grateful thanks
to Maria Elisabetta Forrest for her kind and
generous assistance with my Italian grammar.*

CHAPTER ONE

PASSION was the last thing on Pia Renfern's mind when she approached the row of car-hire booths at Rome's Fiumicino airport preparing to take a massive risk and drive on the wrong side of the road. But sometimes, in a foreign land, things happened beyond the control of the most careful people.

Da Vinci Auto looked the most likely of the hire places. Parking her baggage trolley by the counter, Pia assumed a bright, breezy smile for the clerk. '*Mi scusi, signora,* can you tell me the cost of hiring a car for the day?'

The woman's shrewd gaze appraised Pia right through to her tender Australian conscience, which had only known the left hand side of any road it had ever travelled.

'For one day, *signorina*?'

'Yes, I only need it for the one. Just to get me to Positano.' The clerk's eyebrows arched high, and Pia felt obliged to explain. 'You see, my flight was late and I've missed the bus I was booked on. I'd have caught a train, but with the train strike...' She made a rueful gesture. She tried a smile, but after the stresses of a twenty-four-hour flight, it was a little wobbly. 'I've tried taxis but none of the drivers will agree to take me that far.'

The woman examined all five feet four of Pia from her blonde short cut, down to her blue suede jacket, travel-weary jeans and ankle boots.

'May I see your passport, *signorina*? And your driving authority?'

Pia sensed a presence loom up behind her like a brooding shadow. As she handed over her documents she noticed the clerk's glance flit to somewhere above and beyond her head. For the first time the woman's face burst into beaming smiles. *'Ah, signore. Saro con Lei fra poco.'*

Pia glanced behind. An Italian man was standing there, leaning negligently on the towing handle of his suitcase. He was at least six feet tall, probably seven, with thick brows and intelligent dark eyes that connected at once with hers and gleamed with a disturbing boldness that zinged through her like a chemical infusion.

Pia turned sharply back to the woman. She shouldn't have looked. If there was one thing she wasn't ready for, it was big, lean and hungry and packed with testosterone, however handsome it might appear.

Valentino Silvestri, on the other hand, just flown in from Tunis after co-ordinating Interpol's latest gruelling assault on the narcotics trade, felt a strange frisson prickle the nape of his neck and shiver down his spine.

He willed the pretty blonde to turn around again for another glimpse of her arresting blue eyes. Deprived of the face, he allowed his appreciative gaze to wander further.

Below the hem of her jacket, her blue jeans cupped a luscious little behind as sweetly rounded as an apricot. His mouth watered. *Dio*, how he yearned for a woman.

Pia held her breath while the clerk perused the passport with a frown while at the same time assaulting her keyboard with swift staccato fingers.

The woman glanced up. 'Were you hoping for a large car, *signorina*, or small?'

Relieved the woman was unconcerned about sides of roads, Pia ignored the dark eyes burning through the back of her neck. 'Oh, small. Small will be fine. *Grazie.*'

Her optimism rose. With a bit of luck she could reach her safe haven well before nightfall. Things were starting to look promising, though she had to admit to a few qualms about actually taking the car on the roads once she had it in her possession. Lucky she'd had the forethought to obtain an international licence before she left home just in case of emergencies like this, though her mother had pleaded with her never to use it.

But she was no longer the bundle of nerves she'd been a few months ago when she'd had the post-traumatic stress disorder. If there was one affliction Pia Renfern was now officially free and clear of, it was PTSD in all its insidious, debilitating, creepy manifestations. She was over it, and courage was now her middle name. Just let anyone try to contradict her.

Anyway, driving on the other side of the road couldn't be so hard. Other people did it. Lauren, her cousin, drove all over Italy without mishap. Pia was certain she could manage it if she avoided the super highways and used less popular byways.

Her driving record was pretty good, apart from a few minor parking violations. There was that time she'd had her licence suspended for frequent and incorrigible speeding, but that was ages ago when she'd just passed her test. Lucky the international licence showed nothing of her reckless past.

The woman looked up. 'Where are you wishing to return the car, Miss Renfern?'

'Do you have an office in Positano?'

'No, *signorina*.' The woman's face grew serious. 'Positano has very few spaces for cars. You may perhaps drive to our office in Sorrento then take the bus. Are you familiar with the area?'

'Not exactly. Won't the car have sat nav?'

There was a sudden movement behind her. *'Scusi, signorina.'*

Pia glanced around in surprise. 'Sorry?'

The man stepped forward, his dark eyes glinting with an intent light. Pia's throat dried and a fluttery sensation inhabited her chest. He really *was* handsome, with cheekbones and shadow on his firm, chiselled jaw. His eyebrows bristled with purpose. They were the most stirring she'd ever laid eyes on, while the casual elegance of his black leather jacket, white open-necked shirt and jeans did nothing to diminish the pleasing athleticism of his lean, powerful build.

He was at least a millimetre too close, bearing down on her and sending all her alarm sensors into total chaos. She took a step backwards from those compelling dark eyes and found herself pressed up against the counter.

'I couldn't help overhearing, *signorina*. You are travelling to Positano?' His voice was deep and appealingly accented, despite the seriousness of his tone.

'Yes?'

'Are you aware that the roads near Sorrento are very narrow and built on the edges of cliffs?' His dark eyes scanned her face like a searchlight.

'Well, yes, I suppose. So...?' She could feel her resistance rising to this intrusion. So the roads were narrow. Was he suggesting she wasn't *capable*? She felt her neck grow hot, conscious of the car-hire woman listening to every word with close attention. A stillness seemed to fall on the neighbouring booths, as if their staff, their customers, the entire airport had all paused to listen.

In an effort to dampen the guy's damned cheek, Pia zapped him with a cool smile. 'What's your point, *signore*?'

'The traffic along those roads is heavy and dangerous. Even very experienced drivers from the locality find it so.' His intelligent dark eyes were serious, his hands eloquent. 'Permit me, *signorina*, but I notice that you speak like an Australian. Have you ever before driven a car in a right-hand-traffic situation?'

Guilt crept up Pia's spine. Her entire body warmed, then blazed with it as she felt the car-hire woman's eyes drill a hole through the side of her head. If only she could have lied, but she'd never been good at it, not even to save her life.

'Well, no, maybe I haven't,' she blustered. 'But I know I *can*, and I'm not sure what it has to do with you.'

He shook his head in stern disapproval. 'This is not good. You mustn't try to drive on these roads, especially with the traffic as it will be today with the trains not running. This is what I think would be best. *I* will—'

Before he could go on with his astonishing impertinence, the car-hire woman interjected. '*Scusi*, Miss Renfern. Our apologies, but Da Vinci Auto find we do not have a car for you today.'

'What?' Pia spun about and stared at the woman in outrage. 'Oh, but that's so unfair. You've seen my licence… I'm a qualified driver. This man is a *stranger*. Don't listen to him. What is he to do with me?'

'I am sorry, *signorina*.' Briskly, the woman handed back Pia's credentials. 'Perhaps another car company will help you. However, Da Vinci Auto says no.'

'But—'

'No, and no and no.' The woman folded her arms and sealed her lips with implacable firmness.

Simmering, Pia replaced her documents and gathered her baggage, pausing to cast a glowering glance at the man before she moved off. 'Thanks a lot, *signore*.' She did her best to lace the word with purest strychnine.

His eyes gleamed. '*Prego*. Your safety is important to every Italian.'

She rarely argued with men these days, especially strangers, but some men needed to be argued with. 'I would be much *safer* if I could hire a car.'

Her indignation seemed to amuse the guy. He leaned back against the counter, allowing his thick black lashes to flicker down while his sensual gaze drifted over her with frank appreciation. 'So, so soft…and yet so fierce.' His lean hands demonstrated her softness in the air. She had little doubt it had more to do with her breasts than anything. 'It is a pity,' he continued with phoney sympathy, 'but the *signora* here has made the decision, no doubt for her own reasons.' He shrugged and spread his hands as if he were absolutely innocent in the matter.

This distortion of reality was too much for Pia, confused as it was with messages from his hot smiling eyes, sexy mouth and tanned, elegant hands that were anything *but* innocent. Soft, was she?

She said hotly, 'She made the decision because *you* sowed seeds of doubt in her mind.'

'You think?' His gorgeous brows lifted quizzically. 'She may have been influenced by some weird desire to save lives. But as it happens I'm driving to Positano. I might be able to fit you in. I'm guessing you won't take too much room.' His beautiful hands illustrated just how much room she might take, this time managing to encompass the shape of her hips with what felt to Pia almost like a tangible caress.

She could imagine what he had in mind. He wanted to get her alone in a confined space and run those hard, lean hands all over her body.

If only his voice didn't seep into her veins like a dark intoxicant. At the same time there was that smile in his eyes inviting her to acknowledge an undertow, a distinctly sexual vibration tugging at her like the moon to the tide.

In spite of herself Pia felt a dangerous stir in her blood, then her heart skittered. *Whoa there, girl.* Don't be sucked in by midnight eyes and a lazy smile.

Regrouping her feminine forces, she cast him a crushing look. 'You *wish.*'

She strode coolly away, as coolly as it was possible to pushing a trolley laden with a suitcase and a heavy canvas bag stuffed with easels and painting supplies while feeling his scorching-hot gaze follow her every step of the way.

She walked past the other car-hire booths without wasting her time humbling herself before them. Her reputation was shot with them all now, and there was no way she'd give the guy the satisfaction of watching her being turned away yet again.

The nerve of him. He had to be one of the most intrusive, irritating, interfering, annoying people she'd ever met. Just because he knew he was attractive... Of course he knew. A man that sophisticated always knew.

She was seething all over. He should never have looked at her like that, making her feel so—female. In fact, it was amazing he'd triggered those responses. She'd been numb in that department for so long she couldn't quite believe the sensations were real. It must have been as the doctor had warned. Now that her emotions had come back in full force, every sensation was bound to be stronger, sharper. *Sweeter*, though she squashed that thought. Nothing she felt about him was sweet.

Just before she turned the corner into the next mall though, she couldn't resist sneaking a glance back. He was still there, but to her surprise no longer alone. A middle-aged couple with a teenager had joined him and were exclaiming over him, reaching up to kiss and embrace him like long-lost relatives. She saw him bend to kiss the woman on both cheeks.

Whew. How must that feel?

Resigned to abandoning his interest in the blonde woman for the moment, Valentino pocketed his car keys and braced himself to field a volley of probing queries about his personal life.

As always his uncle and aunt wanted to know too much. Still embarrassed by his divorced status even after all this time, they were forever on the lookout for signs he was about to risk the marital treadmill again.

As if.

He sometimes had the suspicion that his aunt had dreams of him taking up with Ariana again to wipe away the family shame, as though the bitterness had never happened. As though the divorce had no validity.

No use to explain that the twenty-first century had dawned some time back. In his aunt's mind his singularity made him a dangerous loose gun who needed to be nailed down and rigidly secured. His uncle's view appeared slightly different. Possibly tinged with awe, even a little envy.

The old boy winked at him. 'Still playing the field, eh, Tino?'

'That's enough,' his aunt snapped. 'When are you coming home to settle down, Tino?'

They didn't hazard any enquiries about his work. His job as a Criminal Intelligence Officer with Interpol was not an occupation to warm the hearts of family members. They preferred to gloss over it, always slightly on their guards with him for fear he'd be listening to their every word with a view to collecting evidence.

They needn't have worried. He'd run checks on them all and they were depressingly upright and moral.

His aunt began to regale him with the latest on her eldest daughter. Maria was a shining family example. Decently married, blessedly pregnant, in fact on the very verge of delivering them another grandchild as every good son and daughter should. While the couple argued over all the minor details of Maria's health, their youngest son scowled and tried to act as if he didn't belong to them.

Valentino exchanged a sympathetic grin with the boy, musing that, while listening was his speciality, there were times when tuning out was of even more strategic importance.

He was overwhelmed with a sudden longing to escape the grim realities of his life. For a second he allowed himself to imagine how it might have been zooming along the autostrada with the pretty blonde to rest his eyes on, a slim knee to fondle.

His fingers curved into his palm in regret for the silky knee they would never know.

How long had it been since he'd caressed a woman? There must be some left in the world who weren't set on dragging a man to the altar.

Those serious blue eyes, rosy lips and delicate cheekbones in intriguing contradiction to the sprinkling of freckles across her quite charming nose had potential to enchant a man, for a few days at least. There'd been a chemistry, he felt sure. The trip would have been a perfect opportunity to lay the ground-work for a little vacation romance.

He frowned. No doubt she'd receive other offers before the end of the day, though he hoped she wouldn't accept any of them. For her sake he hoped she'd choose the bus. With the degrees of human inventiveness for evil he'd witnessed over the years he began to doubt if any woman should travel alone, anywhere.

He scanned the suspects coming and going around him. How many of these innocent-looking pillars of society were engaged in criminal activity?

It weighed a man down, this constant policing. Lately, wher-ever he looked he saw corruption. Sometimes he wished he could shrug it all off like an unwanted skin. Forget about crime and rid his mind of terrorism threats, narcotics, human traf-ficking, credit-card fraud and the constant thievery of national treasures. Just relax and enjoy a vacation like anyone else. Enjoy a pretty woman and take her at face value.

And what a face. He sighed.

Waking suddenly to his surroundings, Valentino noticed that the car-hire queue had swelled in number, while even more people were flocking to the neighbouring booths. He tapped his uncle's elbow to alert him to the rush, but by the time the old boy inserted himself into the line it was too late.

Da Vinci Auto was all out of cars.

'Per carita,' his uncle wailed, slapping his forehead. 'Now it's a bus strike. First the trains, now the buses. What's the country coming to? What are we to do?'

At once Valentino's thoughts switched to the Australiana. What would *she* do? He felt a twinge of remorse about his intervention, though he'd only acted for the best. It was his duty as a citizen to uphold public safety, surely.

Though if she was stranded he couldn't help feeling some responsibility. He weighed his car keys in his hand.

Pia received the news like a blow.

The drivers were meeting, the harassed attendant explained earnestly to the small angry crowd before the bus link counter. Everything was on hold.

Exactly what Pia didn't want to hear. *On hold* was what her life had been for more than half a year, and she'd come all this way across the world, determined to break out of her security cocoon, plunge back into sweet lovely life and wring from it every last ounce of pleasure and excitement.

None of it could happen until she escaped from the numbing blandness of airport world.

Groaning about what could be a wait of potential *days*, she collapsed onto a chair and closed her eyes. As usual there was a man at the root of her troubles. She should have been cruising along the Amalfi coastline by now. If only she hadn't engaged in conversation with the guy. She should have ignored his eyebrows, never even made eye contact.

Maybe it was an omen and she'd made a terrible mistake agreeing to house-sit for Lauren. Then she chided herself for that backsliding thought.

Concentrate on the positive. She'd come a long way from that timid mouse who'd cowered inside her terrace in Balmain day and night, padlocks on the doors and all the lights turned on. Every night the same predictable curry in the microwave. Every night, her lonely bed all to herself.

She'd made great strides since that first conscious decision to grasp life in both hands and plunge in again with a hopeful heart and positive attitude. Her spirits, her confidence had lifted a thousandfold. How else could she have walked onto the plane? She'd even come round to thinking it was time to chance her luck again with the other species, though she'd be more careful this time.

Where she'd gone wrong had been in allowing herself to fall in love and trust the love to last into the future ad infinitum. Big mistake.

It was time for a brand-new paradigm. Love was a madness that ended in tears. Much better to be fond of someone, love them while they were fun, leave them on a high note. And no more of these slick, fast-talking, sport-obsessed guys who loved a woman when she was well and whole, as long as she looked good enough to flash around at friends' parties.

She'd ensure her next man had a vestige of sensitivity. So he might not be a tall, blond sex-god with rippling muscles. She was prepared, quite prepared, to look for someone less athletic. Big strong men were too domineering, anyway.

Yeah. The more she considered the subject, the more she felt ready for some sweet, gentle guy with a slighter build who didn't much care for sport. Who needed handsome? Handsome men were only too likely to be arrogant, egotistical narcissists who saw women as prey. Fine for the occasional fling, perhaps, the odd wild weekend of passion, but in the long term on a day-to-day basis she'd be much better off with someone who could understand her. Perhaps someone from the arts who shared the creative temperament. A sculptor. Maybe even a musician.

She picked up a newspaper someone had left on the seat and tried to fathom one of the front-page stories with the remnants of her high-school Italian. From what she could make out, some enterprising thief had stolen another little-known painting from a museum in Cairo. A Monet, this time. There was a photo of the picture, which couldn't have done it justice. From its grainy quality she could just make out some reeds and a couple of water lilies.

Her sparse Italian wasn't up to interpreting the finer details, so after a minute she cast the paper aside and lifted her feet to stretch out along the seats with her head on her arm. Closing her eyes, she made herself concentrate on the future.

Beautiful Positano, where no one knew that eleven months ago in the Balmain branch of the Unity Bank a man in a ski mask had shoved a gun into the side of her head and made her believe she was going to die.

Thank heavens for this opportunity to escape to a place where no one would ever dream how for a time that little drama had changed her entire life. What a wimp she'd been for months. One minute there she'd been, swanning through her reckless life with total disregard for what was around the corner, taking pleasure in her man, her friends, her blossoming work, her growing reputation, while the next minute...

Until then she'd never known a thing about stress. It had come as a complete shock to her when, after the incident at the bank, all her mild little anxieties and cautions, the same ones everyone needed to keep themselves alive and well, had crept out of the woodwork and morphed into monstrous great phobias.

Who'd ever have guessed it could happen to a cool sassy femme like herself? Unbelievably, she'd lost her renowned chutzpah and become scared of falling, drowning, crossing the road, being poisoned by unwashed lettuce, eaten by dogs and dying young. And, of course, big strong men in ski masks.

Imagine her, Pia Renfern, up-and-coming landscape painter and portraitist, accepted as a bona fide exhibiting member of the Society, giving into fear. But to be struck by the worst tragedy of all and lose her ability to *paint*.

As always when she thought of it, her stomach churned into a knot. But with a determined effort she fought the nauseous feeling. She needed to be positive and see the glass as half full. The horrible time was past. She was strong again and most of her anxieties had retreated back to their lairs. Only occasionally did one still leap out and surprise her.

Now she only had her painting block to contend with, and, thanks to Lauren, Positano would give her the kick-start she needed. Once there, faced with all that beauty, she felt sure she'd be inspired to paint again.

She'd barely managed five dozy minutes of concentrating on the positive before she felt a looming presence.

She knew who it was. Even before she looked her pulse started an erratic gallop.

She opened her eyes, then had to narrow them to shut out as much of the view as possible. How could black hair, strong brows and deep, dark, glowing eyes be so dazzling?

Her wild pulse registered his mouth. Michelangelo might well have taken pride in having chiselled those meltingly stern, masculine lines. For a second her resolution to only consider slighter, more sensitive men wavered.

Until she remembered. She frowned, then sat up with graceful unconcern. 'Oh, it's you. The man who interferes.'

He inclined his head. 'Valentino Silvestri.'

His eyes were serious now, cool, and though he curled his tongue around the r with devastating charm, his manner was brisk. A charged purposeful energy buzzed in the air around him.

'I'm about to leave for Positano.' He glanced at his watch. A telling movement, because it required him to push up the sleeve of his shirt and reveal his bronzed sinewy wrist. 'Depending on the traffic, I expect to arrive there soon after midday.'

There were black curly hairs on the wrist, and more poking from beneath his cuff. It wasn't too much of a stretch to imagine there might be more on his chest.

With an effort she dragged her glance away. 'Why are you telling me?'

'You need the transportation. I am Italian, and it is the desire of our nation to welcome visitors and make them happy. So...?'

'I doubt if you could make me happy.'

He relaxed and laughed, a low sexy laugh, his white teeth contrasting with his olive tan. 'Ah, *signorina.* You so encourage me to try.' He produced a set of car keys from his jeans pocket and dangled them in front of her. 'At least allow me to make some amends for spoiling your chances to hire the car.'

Ah, now that was better. She started to feel slightly more forgiving. Still, though her body was giving her chaotic signals and her travel options were nil, her response was immediate.

'No, thanks.'

'No? You're sure? Fast car, good driver, safe trip?'

She shook her head.

He was silent a moment, frowning, then a gleam shone in his eyes. 'Did I mention that my uncle, aunt and cousin will be coming along?' With a gesture he directed her gaze to the family group she'd seen hugging him a few minutes earlier. They stood several metres away by the escalator with a pile of luggage, looking her way with avid curiosity. Even the sullen boy seemed halfway interested.

'Oh, them?' Pia appraised them, doubtfully at first, then with her heart leaping up in sudden hope. 'Really?'

A few months ago being crammed into a car with a bunch of strangers, forced to make small talk, would have been her idea of hell, but today... The family looked to be the essence of safe, solid respectability. Was this her chance to escape from the airport and break out into the world of grass, sky and fresh air?

She eyed Valentino, awaiting her response with apparent patience. What was his motive? Remorse? Something else? 'I don't know... Though I guess... Are you sure—it wouldn't be an intrusion?'

He made an amused grimace. 'It would be a relief.'

'They won't mind?'

'They'll be fascinated.'

'I wouldn't want to impede your conversation with your family, or...or your—your privacy in any way...'

'You couldn't if you tried.'

'Oh, well, then. Thanks.' She stood up, smoothed down her clothes, picked up her bag. 'Thanks very much. Though you—you do know this is just a lift, er—Valentino. Nothing more than that.'

His brows lifted. '*Scusi, signorina?* What else would it be?' He tilted his head with an expression of polite inquiry, and she felt a pang. Had she been crass to spell it out?

'I was just—ensuring that you—understand...'

His expression grew grave and quite dignified, as if she was insulting his honour, his reputation, his very heart and soul. She nearly had to pinch herself. Wasn't this the same bold devil who'd been flirting with her only half an hour since?

'Look, I—I just need to be clear you *know* that...this is not a pick-up.'

Looking totally mystified, he drew his black brows together. 'A pick-up. What is this pick-up? Is it an Australian thing?'

She flushed and shook her head. 'No, no. It's... Look, it's when...'

It homed in on her at last that despite his beautiful accent up until now he had really quite excellent English. She stared suspiciously at his solemn, intent face, noting the sly glint in his brilliant dark eyes. 'You know exactly what I mean, don't you?'

He grinned in acknowledgement, then broke into a laugh, his eyes lighting with amusement at her chagrin.

'I might know, *signorina.*'

'Fine.' She let out an exasperated breath. '*Well.* So long as you understand I'm accepting this lift purely as a—a—an emergency and I have no intention of being taken for a ride. And it's Pia.'

He shot her a keen glance, then his luxuriant black lashes swept smilingly down.

'Pia,' he echoed. '*Bella.* I am charmed.'

He was charmed. Well, she might have been a little that way herself, although at the same time she was churned up, confused and irritated. Did he think a woman's concern for her personal safety was a joke?

She took the hand he offered her, but briefly. As soon as his hard palm brushed hers her overreactive skin cells leaped like flying fish on ecstasy. And her hand continued to tingle as she trundled her baggage beside him to where the family waited by the escalator.

He said, 'So long as *you* understand that I will be doing the driving.' His eyes gleamed, but there was a definiteness in his tone that brooked no argument.

'What a surprise.' She rolled her eyes, while inside her giddy pulse was rushing like storm water.

CHAPTER TWO

VALENTINO SILVESTRI drove fast, switching from lane to lane and cutting a path into tiny impossible crevices amongst the traffic with blithe disregard for the nerves of his passengers. Pia clung to her seat belt, enduring the aunt's penetrating voice and trying not to dwell on the possibilities of dying young.

The aunt had directed the seating arrangement, guarding her menfolk by steering her husband into the front passenger seat and planting her solid self in the back between Pia and the sulky boy. Pia envied the boy his earphones, but resisted retreating to her own for fear of causing offence.

During a rare lull in the conversation Valentino's deep dark eyes sought Pia's briefly in the rear vision mirror and he said in his ravishingly accented voice, 'So, Pia, why have you abandoned Australia for Italy?'

'I'm here to house-sit for my cousin.' Pia had to raise her voice a little to be heard. 'Lauren's a photographer. She's gone to Nepal with a film crew to shoot a snow leopard. Maybe you know her. Lauren Renfern?'

Valentino shook his head. 'Is she a recent arrival? I haven't been in Positano for some time.'

'She's lived there just over a year.'

'There are so many newcomers now we don't know our own town,' the aunt chimed in. 'But you will be very happy. Of course, you will go to Pompeii. Herculaneum is another very fine site. And you must join the climb to Vesuvius, shouldn't she, *amore*? Vesuvius is a marvellous experience.'

'And Capri,' her husband added, turning to encourage Pia. 'All the *turisti* go to Capri. You will love it.'

'Shh,' the aunt hissed, poking her husband and nodding towards Valentino with a frown. In a murmur she added, 'Have you no respect?'

Pia glanced at Valentino in surprise. Why shouldn't Capri be mentioned, or was it the fact of her being a tourist that was the trouble? She saw his sensuous mouth tighten a little in the mirror, but that was the only sign he gave of having heard the aunt's murmur. A moment later Pia's gaze accidentally collided with his, and his dark eyes were so compelling, so sensual she forgot everything except the sudden mad rushing in her veins.

That was why it was such a shock when, just as the first glimpses of the Bay of Napoli hoved into view, the aunt received a call on her cell phone and startled everyone with the announcement that her beloved Maria had started in labour. It was an emergency, the agitated woman declared. She was sorry, but there was no help for it. The journey must be halted and they must speed to her daughter's side at once.

There was no option but to alter the itinerary, so at the first available exit they diverted from the autostrada and drove into Napoli, where Valentino deposited the family with all their baggage in the entrance to Maria's apartment building.

With their departure a blissful silence descended over the car. While Valentino said his farewells, Pia stayed in her seat, staring out at the busy, ancient, narrow street, craning up at the tall buildings, a sudden tension in her nerves. An anticipation.

What now? Now she would be alone with him?

She saw his tall frame turn to stroll back and a shiver thrilled down her spine.

Valentino paused with his hand on the door handle. A curi-

ous sensation charged his blood. His passenger hadn't moved
from her corner. Was she so wary of him?

With measured calm he got in, reached for the ignition, then
turned to examine her.

Her blue eyes met his frankly, a little defiantly. He felt his
blood quicken. He had no wish to make her feel vulnerable,
but she was so pretty. He'd hardly be human not to feel excited
by the situation.

Pia sensed the air tauten. Suddenly she felt as if she were
hanging over the edge of a cliff.

He lifted his brows. 'So...are you staying over there?' His
eyes were coolly amused, questioning, then he pointed at the
seat next to his.

On a surge of adrenaline, Pia overruled the sudden tension
in her limbs. She reasoned that men were probably like horses
and dogs. The last thing a woman should do was to give out
some crazy vibe of being nervous. As soon as she acknowledged the threat, the threat would become real.

What was there to be nervous about, anyway? Just because
he'd looked at her once or twice as if she were a strawberry
tartlet didn't mean he was planning to speed her to the nearest
lonely bush track to have his ruthless way with her. He'd hardly
engineered the current situation. It was fate who had gone to
such great trouble to arrange it, bringing on babies and all.

So long as fate didn't get carried away. So long as *he* didn't.

As she slid into the seat next to his and he reached across
to assist her in finding the seat buckle her heightened senses
caught the faintest tang of clean, spicy masculinity. She secured
the seat belt, taking care not to brush his fingers. Smoothly,
casually.

'Bene.'

Valentino's eyes were drawn to a tiny flickering pulse disturbing the smooth skin of her temple. His fingers twitched
with a sudden urge to reach out and stroke her, but he restrained
the impulse.

He realised it was only natural she should feel some concern. What woman wouldn't? He was a man, after all. Practically a wild animal. There would be no use in telling her he was the safest guy on the planet and upholder of the laws of one hundred and eighty-eight nations.

He considered various things he might say to reassure her, and discarded them all as being likely to be counterproductive.

Accelerating into the traffic stream, he worked at keeping the conversation at an easy flow. 'Sorry about the change in plans. *Bambini* make their own rules, apparently.' He indicated the dash clock. 'Not much more than an hour to go now. Just enough time for us to introduce ourselves properly.'

Pia read reassurance in the smile he flashed her. He was making an effort, she realised. Either to ensure she felt comfortable, or to lull her into a false sense of security.

'So tell me,' he said in his velvet voice, 'what do you plan to do in Positano?'

Stay calm and pleasant, Pia thought, eyeing his handsome jaw with its hint of shadow, his hands, casual on the wheel. No matter how smooth and polished, remember he's one of the wolvish tribe. Keep him on an even keel. Don't antagonise him.

Her hands clasped themselves in her lap. 'See the sights. Soak up the beauty.'

'Ah. You are on vacation?'

She nodded. 'And you, Valentino—do you live in Positano or are you just visiting?'

Valentino hesitated. Too much information would inevitably lead to him divulging his job to her. As soon as he did that she'd make all sorts of false assumptions about him and close up. It had happened too many times before with potential playmates. Mention Interpol and they vanished over the horizon like smoke. Tracking and pursuing high-class criminals was a grim business, more painstaking than romantic, but it was time his organisation received a sexier press.

He lifted his hands in acknowledgement of her question.
'My family home is there but I work—elsewhere.'

'Oh?'

'Sì.' He engineered a quick diversion. 'I think you will enjoy
Positano. It's very small, but you shouldn't have any trouble
finding entertainment. Are you adventurous, Pia?'

Pia looked quickly at him. His glance was searching, smiling with just the hint of a sexy challenge, and her heart lurched
into a higher gear. Of course he'd have used the word deliberately. He was a man, wasn't he?

'No, I'm not,' she said, pouring iced water on any attempt
to flirt. 'Not at all.'

'No?' He lifted his thick black brows. 'That's not what I
would have thought.' A smile flickered at the corners of his
sexy mouth. A meditative, sophisticated smile.

What did that mean? Pia wondered. Had he somehow di-
vined the old courageous, indestructible Pia she used to be?
Were elements of her former carefree self peeping out like a
tart's petticoat, or was this merely a seduction technique?

'You have travelled across the world all by yourself. I would
think that took some courage.' His dark eyes were all at once
surprisingly kind and sincere, and Pia realised she'd misinter-
preted his intention. 'No?'

She allowed him a cautious smile and his eyes lit with a
warmth that made her breath catch.

'Oh, well...I guess.'

She gave a breezy shrug as though her journey had been
nothing much, though the truth was she'd been a nervous wreck
for the first three thousand miles. Lucky they'd flown into
darkness and the plane's blinds had been drawn.

'It's as well to be fit in Positano,' he went on, 'but you don't
need to be too adventurous to enjoy hiking the mountain trails
or exploring the grottoes. You must find yourself a guide. If
you go to the tourist office they will help you.'

Pia felt ashamed of her low suspicions.

It just went to show she should get over herself. She was far too jumpy and ready to think the worst of every man she met. Clearly, it was time to let go of her angst and start to take people as she found them. *Men*, as she found them. They couldn't all be thinking of sex and violence *all* the time.

She sat back and allowed some of her tension to slacken a little. Here was a guy who'd been kind enough to come to her rescue, and all she could do was search for signs he was keen to jump her bones.

And not just any old plain guy, as it happened. The more she saw of him, the more convinced she was of his drop-dead gorgeousness. She stole another glance. He looked so relaxed, his long limbs comfortably disposed in the sleek auto. He'd rolled his shirt sleeves back a little and his arms were as lean and tanned as she'd imagined. Sinewy. His collar opening revealed more of his olive-toned skin, the strong bronzed column of his neck.

From an artistic viewpoint, the composition was fine. In fact, it was hard to take her eyes off him. The chiselled lines of his profile ravished her more with every slight movement of his head. Not, she reminded herself, that she was especially looking for chiselled. Or even looking.

Valentino felt her gaze flicker over him and his blood hummed with a buoyant little charge. The chemistry was fizzing. And *Grazie a Dio* for that smile. A smile on a mouth so luscious was almost as good as a kiss, though a kiss would be highly desirable. Suddenly he felt glad to be alive and free and a mere mortal man.

For the first time in ages his office at the bureau, the meetings with his team, the constant policing demands from forces around the world seemed a million miles away.

Added to that, the sun was shining, the car handling well, he was flying down the autostrada with a blonde and the thaw was under way.

If he could tempt her into that smile again, in no time at all

the conversation would segue into some light and flirty rep-
artee and Miss Pia Renfern would be ready for some real adventure.

'Have your family always lived in Positano, Valentino?' Pia
said politely to break the silence.

'For centuries, as far as we can count. My parents are no
longer alive but my grandfather's still there.' He bathed her in
a dark gleaming glance that seeped into her veins like old co-
gnac. 'Have yours always lived in Sydney?'

'Not quite always. Some of us may have managed one or
two centuries. I'm sorry about your parents.'

Mesmerised by the amber highlights in his brilliant dark
eyes, she felt her instincts plunge into warring turmoil.
Somehow, while her internal security centre had been all for
raising the alarm barriers high and keeping him at a very safe
distance, another part of her was at risk of gaining the upper
hand. An alarmingly female part that was softening and being
drawn to him like a fridge magnet.

She still felt perched on a precarious edge, but the quality
of the edge had changed.

He said casually, 'Isn't there some Aussie guy back there
missing his *bella ragazza*?'

'Not especially.' There were some things a woman wasn't
about to confess. It wasn't much to boast that the Aussie guy
she'd once called the love of her life had bumped her for a
trainee accountant with lank hair.

'Amazing.' His dark eyes scanned her face. 'No wonder
they can't play the beautiful game.'

'What game is that?'

He stared incredulously at her, then his gaze grew pitying.
'*Per carita*. This is a tragedy.'

'Is it some Italian thing?' she said innocently.

'*Mio Dio.*' He threw up his hands, though luckily they connected with the wheel again before the car veered off course.
'*Football*. Have any of you Aussies heard of *football*?'

She grinned to herself, then at him. As if every woman in Australia hadn't been battered into insensibility with every sporting contest ever devised by man.

His eyes narrowed as he realised she'd been kidding him, then his lean face broke into a laugh. Like the sun breaking out. His eyes were alight and she was devastated, her veins once again melting. His laugh was infectious and her tension eased down another twenty levels. Nothing like a moment of shared humour with a gorgeous Neapolitan to help a girl relax.

He gazed at her with friendly mockery. 'Lucky you have come to a civilised country where you can start to learn how to live. How long do you stay?'

'However long it takes.'

'To do what?'

'Oh. Well...' She gestured. 'I mean, however long Lauren's away, or...or whatever happens.' Such as how long it took to get her painting back.

'Let's hope Lauren stays away a long time.' The words hung in the air, unsettling, provocative.

She made no reply and Valentino wondered ruefully if he'd blundered. He didn't want to rush things. It wasn't any quick on-road seduction he had in mind. Not that he couldn't be tempted.

Involuntarily his heart quickened at the maverick thought. *Sacramento.* Where had that come from? He deserved to be shot. He was a disciplined man. A professional warrior against crime, a defender of the innocent.

Regardless of how soft and curvy and feminine she was, how achingly close and accessible, there were standards of behaviour an honourable man never contravened.

He cast her a sidelong glance.

Her brow was slightly wrinkled. He saw her bite her lower lip and a pang went through him. He forced his eyes back to the road. *Dio*, her lips were so plump and rosy.

Pia had the feeling his antennae were up and paying close

attention to everything she said. She just hoped he didn't ask too many prickly questions about her work. She so hated to lie. Lies always caught you out in the end, and who was to say she mightn't run into him again after today, since they were both heading for the same town?

If there was one thing she didn't want to have to admit to anyone, it was how her meltdown had almost wiped her out.

Losing Euan had been bad enough, but it was her career that had been the worst casualty. In a way, losing her ability to paint had been like losing her identity.

The block had been terrifying, even worse than losing her desire, though it was that loss that had most concerned Euan. He'd thought he was the one suffering from deprivation. For her, failing to paint was like failing to *breathe*.

Thank God the nightmare was in the past and her emotions had whooshed back in full force. It gave her hope that her creative flow was on the verge of recovery. She'd had glimmers lately, though so far none had carried through into any successful work. As for her desire...

Irresistibly her gaze was drawn to linger on Valentino's long, smooth fingers tightening around the gear lever, the powerful thigh muscles stretching the fabric of his jeans.

That burning little question was now wide open.

He turned his dark gaze on her. 'Where does she live, your cousin?'

'In the Via del Mare. She scored a fantastic contract with a television company, so she bought an apartment. Do you know the street?'

His brows lifted. 'Must have been a fantastic contract. I know it well. You and I could be neighbours. Convenient, wouldn't you say?' He cast her a gleaming glance that seeped into her tissues like absinthe. 'Do you like to travel?'

'I'm almost ashamed to confess this is my first time. Overseas, that is.' She cast him a glance.

'Your *first*?' Both his hands lifted from the wheel. Briefly again, thank goodness. '*Molto bene.* You chose the best place to visit. Your first time needs to be—exceptional. Don't you agree?'

She looked quickly at him, met his gleaming glance, seduction in the smile lurking at the corners of his mouth, and her heart jolted. It had barely slotted back into place when he said, 'What sort of work do you do?'

'All sorts. Part-time mainly.' She started to wonder if there was ever a stone he left unturned when he met someone for the first time. 'Is—is this air conditioning working?' She moistened her lips. She felt his dark questioning gaze turn her way and added quickly, 'What's *your* work, Valentino?'

He reached to change the air setting, and his eyes were all at once screened by his luxuriant black lashes. 'I work for a multi-national company. We do many things...communications, data collection and analysis... We liaise with local companies to help them maximise the success of their operations.'

Whatever that meant. There was something smooth about the words, as if he'd said them exactly the same way a hundred times. Pia eyed him. He was so fit and athletic, he exuded the coiled energy of an action man rather than some desk jockey.

'In an office, you mean?'

His reply was immediate. 'Sometimes. Mostly I'm required to travel.'

'Where are you based?'

'Lyon, though it changes. Milano, Roma, Athens. What did you say is the part-time work you do?'

Back to that. He wasn't just gorgeous, he was tenacious. And there she'd been, hoping he wouldn't besiege her with questions. 'Oh, you know. Office work, restaurants when I have the need for extra cash. You—you must spend a lot of time away from home. Don't you miss Positano?'

'Every day. I wish I could be there more. Though perhaps I enjoy it the more because I see so little of it.' He glanced at her, his dark disturbing gaze caressing her face. 'It is a pity to tire yourself of something you love, don't you think?'

She sighed. 'That's not how life works for me. I always throw myself into the things I love to the max.' Overboard, some people had accused her of being. No doubt it was true. She always had to love things too much. People. Loving them. Trusting them. Believing they loved her. At least, that was how she used to be. Before the bank incident.

'Usually, that is,' she amended, not wanting to give a false impression of her current state.

'Ah. The best kind of woman.' His eyes met hers, sensual, teasing. 'What are they, then? Your passions?'

She took a moment to think, then counted them off on her fingers. 'Beauty. Art. Music.' She shrugged. 'Friendship, of course.'

He grinned. 'Add food and wine to the list and you'll be talking like an Italian.'

She laughed, carried along by his good humour and with the sudden hopeful conviction that passion must still survive intact somewhere, in some part of her.

'And you, Valentino? Tell me yours.'

His thick lashes flickered and he inclined his head a little. 'Beauty, certainly. Honesty. Integrity in public life. Ah, let me think. The sea.'

'The sea?'

'*Sì.*' He gestured. 'I was a *carabiniere* attached to the navy before...what I am doing now.'

She glanced at him in surprise. 'Isn't the Carabinieri the police?'

'It is and it isn't. It is a—military service in its own right. Have you heard of the US marines?'

She nodded. 'Of course.'

'Well, some *carabinieri* are a part of the military forces— similar to the marines. I was with the navy. At heart I am a sailor.'

Wow. She could see why he was built like an athlete. In spite of her inclination to only admire gentle, more artistic men from now on she couldn't help feeling impressed. The very name *carabinieri* had such a swashbuckling ring to it.

'A simple sailor.' She flashed him a smile.

'Very simple.' The glance he flashed back was anything *but* simple. Sophisticated, perhaps. Experienced. Steeped in the seductive arts, definitely. But simple? No.

All at once she was finding it hard to breathe, but in a pleasant way. An exhilarated way. She reflected that pre-bank she'd always enjoyed a flirty conversation with a lovely guy. It was one of the pleasures of life, sussing out the romantic attitudes of the other species. But *post*-bank...

It was as if that part of her had closed down, the flirty part that loved playing the game of advance and retreat in the war of the sexes. With a sudden surge of excitement she realised that today she was reacting quite like her old self. The old Pia Renfern was alive and well, though maybe a little dusty from disuse. Perhaps it just needed a certain kind of stimulus to activate it.

The sort who kept the adrenaline charge in her bloodstream and made her toes curl up.

The fantastic realisation she was back to normal, she was actually enjoying a man's company and feeling like a sexual being again at long, long last, might have gone to her head. She couldn't deny feeling pleasantly dizzy and powerfully feminine. She wanted to stretch all her muscles and purr like a cat. How gorgeous was it to be a woman?

'Are you so passionate, then, Pia?' He didn't look at her, his eyes were on the road, but the velvet challenge in his voice told her what their expression was likely to be.

'When I truly want something.' She half lowered her lashes. 'And you?'

'*Very* passionate,' he said, his voice deepening while the hot gleam in his dark eyes melted her to her ankles. *'Molto molto appassionato.'*

The music of his rich musical Italiano oozed down inside her like an aphrodisiac. Heat washed through her along with sudden thrilling visions of being wrapped in his powerful arms on some lamplit bed, his sleek bronzed body locked with hers, hot, hard and virile.

In chaos she turned her face away, breathless, her heart thumping. She mustn't get carried away. What if she inadvertently encouraged him to expect something?

He said casually, 'Do you have connections in Positano, apart from your cousin?'

'Not really. Oh, there are some friends of Lauren's who live on Capri who might look me up, if they remember. It would be lovely if they did. *Capri.*' She gave a little shiver. To think she might meet actual residents of that fabled island. 'Is it as lovely as they say?'

He hesitated, and his brows lowered slightly. 'It is—*bella*, certainly.'

He didn't sound overwhelmed, but then where in the world did people truly appreciate the treasures in their own back yard?

Her glance fell on his olive-tanned hands, unsullied by any wedding band. 'Do you have family in Positano besides your aunt and uncle?'

He nodded, 'My grandfather. He's a sweet old guy.' He smiled and gestured. 'We are—*simpatico.*'

His voice softened and she warmed to the honest affection in his tone. Family ties were important signals about a man. Obviously there was no woman keeping the home fires burning. Not in Positano anyway. Not that it had anything to do with her. But it couldn't hurt to find out if he had one somewhere else.

She'd always enjoyed delving into a life, glimpsing the man behind the face she sought to portray. Her father had always said it was the most important part of a portraitist's arsenal. But Valentino Silvestri didn't give her the chance to dig far. He kept turning the spotlight neatly around to her.

'Tell me about you, Pia. Who is in your life? A beautiful girl like you?'

Beautiful, was he kidding? If *she* was beautiful, then beauty didn't count for a row of beans. It was coolness, calm and strength that mattered or people walked away. Well, that was her experience.

'For instance,' he said smoothly, 'have you ever been married?'

Pia glanced at him in some surprise. 'How old do you think I am? Ask me that in thirty years' time. I'll start to think about it then.'

A smile touched his sexy mouth and lingered there. 'And in the meantime…?'

As she drank in the strong, chiselled bones of his face it came to her with a thrill of excitement that if she'd had some charcoal handy she could have taken down those bones in a flash. Almost unconsciously she angled her body more his way.

'You know what I think, Valentino?'

'What do you think?' The corners of his mouth edged up further. He sent her a warm, piercing glance and the air grew heady.

'You're a very nosy guy.'

His eyes were amused, sensual. 'Too curious?'

'*Way* too curious. But since you're interested, I take life as I find it. And for your information I come from an ordinary background of wonderful people. I have a mother, a brother and a sister. Uncles, aunts, cousins, the whole thing.'

'No boyfriend? Fiancé?'

'Tsk, tsk.' She shook her head. 'Haven't you *noticed*?' She waved her ringless left hand at him. 'What sort of a detective are you?'

He laughed. 'Clearly not very good. So you might as well

tell me everything. Let me think... Start with the month and year of your birth.'

Pia stared incredulously at him. 'Honestly. You are *relentless*. All right, I'm a Virgo and I'm twenty-six. Satisfied? On the shelf, you might say.' She smiled. 'And I'm guessing you're a *much* older man of the world than that. *Molto*.'

'Molto,' he agreed, smiling. 'A whole thirty-five.' She waited for him to expand on his partner status, but he said nothing. A few more moments ticked by while she racked her brains for a way to ask without sounding madly interested, then he shot her a teasing, sensual glance. 'You aren't interested to know if *I* am on the shelf?'

'Should I be?'

'Then you're not.' He made it sound like a statement, though his voice was silken.

'Well, I am *now*.' She let her lashes flutter down. 'But only because you brought it up.'

He laughed. 'Ah, it's so sexy talking to a clever woman.' He hesitated a second, then said, *'Grazie a Dio* at this moment in time I'm a single man and my conscience is clear.'

She glowed inside. Though truly, feeling so fantastically exhilarated by a little conversational skirmish with a man she'd just met who was dripping with sexual possibilities probably meant her conscience should be anything *but* clear.

But it felt lovely to be admired, to receive hot slumberous glances more intense than the norm, which sometimes included her mouth as well as her eyes, or slid to her throat. It sparked up her blood and made her feel like a desirable woman again, and maybe she flirted a little. Once or twice.

The vegetation had changed. There were fig trees, olive groves and steep hillsides terraced with orchards of lemon and peach, while the warm spring air was scented with the fragrances of wild verbena and basil. The road became increasingly narrow, and soon there were high cliffs on one side and glimpses of sea on the other. So Valentino hadn't exaggerated the danger, after all. The traffic was constant, interspersed with tourist buses and heavy lorries.

She began to feel deeply thankful not to be driving. Truly, she could have kissed that car-hire woman. While most of her fears had long since retreated, she still wasn't so good with heights.

'The road gets even narrower on the other side of Sorrento,' he said. 'We call it the *Nastro Azzurro*, what you would call the Blue Ribbon. You'll know why when you see it.' He growled an exclamation. 'Some of these guys should be locked up. Where are the traffic cops when you need them?' He took his hands from the wheel to gesticulate at a car pelting towards them, replacing them barely in time to swerve the car to safety. 'Look.' He gestured. 'Vesuvius again.'

'Fantastic,' she gasped, her heart all at once in her throat, not daring to look at the views. 'Does this car have airbags?'

'I believe so. Though one can never be sure they will work until the moment of impact.' He smiled and she forced herself to manufacture one for him.

She must try to stop talking to him. It was too dangerous. On every level.

Sorrento was beautiful, the old picturesque town spilling over cliff walls. Every vista was a thrill to Pia's eye, and she wished they could have lingered there and explored those pretty streets and looked behind the bougainvilleaed walls.

Conversation trickled off once they were out of the town. The road reduced to a narrow ribbon of continuous sharp curves and switchbacks, a mere ledge along a cliff face, and surely not wide enough for two small cars to pass, let alone the tourist buses and trucks lumbering along, though Valentino negotiated the blind hairpins with confidence.

Through Pia's window the sea called with breathtaking views across the bay, though she was too conscious of the cliff edge and its lack of a reassuring barrier to enjoy it. She could barely permit herself to look.

Admit it, she was scared, but *not panicking*. She hadn't panicked for months, and she wouldn't panic now in front of Valentino Silvestri.

As they passed through tiny villages clinging to the cliff face she sat taut, hands clenched, and concentrated on breathing.

'…Pia?'

She came to herself with a shock, realising he'd been speaking to her. For how long? She felt a stab of dismay. How much of herself had she betrayed? He glanced at her again, a crease between his brows.

'Sorry?' she said. 'What—what did you say?'

His frown intensified. 'I was asking if you feel okay?'

'Oh, I do. Sure. Fine.' It was just that her breathing often grew shallow when suspended over a couple of thousand feet of cliff in the presence of a sexy man.

Not long afterwards, a bend in the road revealed a lay-by. Valentino swung the car in under some trees and parked. There was a small sharp silence, then he said gently, 'You can stop clutching the seat now. Come. You need some fresh air. Let me show you the view.'

CHAPTER THREE

HER legs might have been unwilling, but Pia would have made them work even if all their bones had been broken. She dragged herself from the car and walked with Valentino across the leafy grass, barely even faltering when they approached the lookout.

The air was dry, hot in the sun, and aromatic with rosemary and other wild scents.

She gripped the stone balustrade with gratitude, though her throat was dry. The view was indeed spectacular, and when the solidity of cement and earth under her hands and feet had worked to settle her vertigo stole the breath from her lungs. Rugged cliff faces and blue, blue sea, misting into infinite sky. Deeper, more intense blue than the human mind could fathom. Indigo into cobalt, aquamarine and turquoise at the edges.

She could do this, she reasoned with herself. Even though they were up so high at least her feet were on solid ground and she had a big strong man beside her who wasn't wearing a ski mask.

Oh, God, why think of that now?

She concentrated on breathing in the blue, allowing its healing qualities into her soul until her heart slowed its irrational racing and she felt herself start to relax. Valentino was leaning on the balustrade, his white shirt-opening cutting a bronzed V, his sleeves rolled up a little, forearms naked to the sun, the image of cool, sexy masculinity.

Cool, but if she could have painted him, the colours would have seared the page.

'You see those little isles out there?' She followed his gaze to where jagged fingers pointed from the sea, piercing the blue haze. 'Remember Ulysses and the sirens who lured the sailors?'

'*That's* the place?' She cleared the croakiness from her throat.

'Yes. And just poking out from that corner of the cliff you see Capri.'

'Oh,' she exclaimed, her voice back to natural. 'It's beautiful.' And she truly meant it. It was beyond beautiful. It was heaven.

He angled himself to gaze at her and the sun found gold and amber glimmers in the depths of his eyes. 'Better now?' There was concern in his voice, and the lines of his chiselled, sensuous mouth were grave.

'I'm fine, truly. I don't know what happened. You shouldn't have worried.' She hardly dared look at him for fear of seeing the curl of contempt she'd once surprised on Euan's mouth when she'd revealed her nervousness.

'You were white.'

She shrugged it off. 'Oh, well, I'm probably overtired. I have been travelling for thirty-six hours. It's only natural I should be a bit pale.'

His eyes flickered to her mouth. 'Not that pale. But you've improved a little. Now your lips are pink.' He moved closer, touched them with his knuckle. 'Like cherries.'

Her heart made a deep lurch in her chest, and he bent and touched her lips with his, a gentle, exploratory friction. It took her by surprise, in truth. Her mad, pounding pulse took off, and she would have stopped the tingling kiss, she really would, except that her lips fell into a sort of divine enchantment. He pulled her close and her hands reached for his shoulders, his ribs, his thick black hair.

Oh, the bliss of being held gently by a hard man. His peppery spice filled her head, and the taste of him, so masculine yet in some way unique, ignited her senses until she was drunk, and for seconds she came close to abandoning herself to his possession.

He gathered her close to his lean solid body and kissed her with a sizzling, sexy, melting heat, titillating the insides of her mouth with his tongue, drugging her brain with the sexual narcotic and razing her to the ground.

She sank into him, stroking him, her body thrilling to his arousing touch.

His smooth hands slid to her breasts and a wild flame of desire flared up in her. Instantly she felt conscious of losing control. At the same time awareness of the implacable power of his big, steel-hard physique sent a choking panic jackknifing through her insides.

She shoved at his powerful chest and broke free from his arms.

'No, don't,' she said hoarsely, panting. 'Not this.'

'Cosa?'

He was staring at her with a strange expression, as though seeing something unexpected in her face. It was infuriating, and she hastened to cover up whatever it had been.

'I—I don't want to be kissed, do you understand?' She was breathing fast. Anger and arousal seethed with equal potency in her bloodstream. For God's sake, what was she doing? Here she was with a perfect stranger on a hellish road in the middle of what looked and smelled like heaven on earth, and for a moment she'd actually come close to getting carried away and letting herself go.

She must have lost her senses.

Blinking as though stunned, he stared at her with eyes that blazed molten. 'I did not—' His voice was thicker and deeper than a Gulf Oil gusher. 'I did not *intend*... This was just... I wanted to comfort you.'

'Oh, to *comfort* me. Please.'

A flush touched his lean cheeks. He said something intense in flowing Italian accompanied by a proud gesture that made it clear he felt stung by her accusation. The trouble was, even in her anger, those lilting, lyrical words, so eloquent of denial, expressed in his deep voice seeped into her bloodstream and threatened to undermine her.

She hardened herself against them and said in a low voice, 'I don't *need* comforting. Anyway, this was not what I'd call comfort. This was a man taking advantage of a woman.'

His head jerked back.

The ferocity of her words surprised even herself. Since the bank incident, she'd taken care to avoid riling members of the opposite sex. As soon as her bold words escaped from her mouth her cowardly heart jumped into her throat and cringed.

He stared at her, frowning, his eyes glittering. 'I am not the sort of man who takes advantage of a woman.' All at once his accent was very pronounced. 'Holding you, kissing you even, seemed like a—a—natural response to your distress. I was intending merely to—soothe you.'

The flush on his sculpted cheekbones deepened on those last words, as if he realised himself how lame they sounded.

'Oh, that's what they all say.'

His eyes flashed. '*Mio Dio*, what sort of guy do you think I am?' He made a small move in her direction, and despite her bravado an involuntary lurch in her guts drove her back a step.

Shock smote his tense, handsome face and he held up his hands. 'Pia… You have no need to feel afraid. I am a civilised man, *perdio*. I do not assault women. Far from it.'

'I'm not *afraid*,' she said sharply, though in fact her blood was thundering in her ears and she was trembling like an aspen. 'Just—disappointed, that's all. I have had a long, long trip. You're a total stranger and I'm not in any mood to be kissing anyone.' Her voice wobbled on the last word, to her utter shame.

But his assurances on the assault issue began to sink in. She started to feel less severely threatened, and as her confidence rose the strength of her anger intensified, and her need to express it.

'You shouldn't have assumed I wanted to kiss you.'

'Okay, okay...' He threw up his hands, muttering in melodic Italiano then switching to English. 'You don't need to explain.'

'I'm not explaining.' And she wasn't, not really. It was just that she felt all wound up and needed to vent her feelings. 'I'm—mortified that you think I'm the sort of woman who would encourage such...such...free and easy...' She made a wordless gesture.

'Kissing.'

'As if any time a man finds a woman on a lonely road he should seize the opportunity. As if this is what *I* was cut out for. To be kissed by a man. Any man who feels like it, any old tick of the clock. All right, Pia, I like the look of you so I'll kiss you. As if I should *enjoy...*'

He'd been listening with close attention, but at that his black lashes swept down to conceal a sudden gleam in his eyes. 'And yet for a few moments there I had the distinct impression you *did* enjoy. You were so very, very responsive. When I held you in my arms I could feel the thrill rippling through your vibrant body. I can feel it still, in my arms, all through my body, all the way to my bones.'

It was her turn to flush. Her conscience pricked, and to make matters worse the very nature of the words he'd used were in some way arousing.

'Oh, rubbish.' She gave a cool, angry laugh and turned away to hide her burning cheeks. 'There was no thrill. The only thing rippling through me was anger.'

She started to walk across the clearing towards the car. She felt all raw inside, as if she were in the wrong somehow and had treated him unfairly, when all the time *he* was the one who had kissed *her*. She supposed if the case made it to court he'd accuse her of flirting with him on the journey.

But what was flirting, after all? A binding contract?

He caught up with her and said stiffly, 'I'm sorry to have distressed you, Pia. If I had realised when you were moaning in my arms—'

'Oh, what, *moaning*? I was not.' Blushing furiously, she turned away.

'*Sì, sì*, I heard you moan.' His voice thickened. 'When you did that it made me so *hot* for you. *Molto molto caldo.*'

The words affected her against her will, coursing through her like a hot tingling aphrodisiac, and with a spurt of sudden anger she spun around to face him. 'Stop this, Valentino. Please. There's no use talking about it.' Gazing at his gorgeous face, so dark and intense, so focused on her, all at once she felt breathless, furious, ready to strike. 'Don't say another word.'

He threw up his hands. 'Okay, okay. Don't be upset. I am not one of these guys who argue and force themselves upon women. You have said no more and no more is how it shall be. Nothing more. *Niente.*'

She strode on, wishing she weren't so *conscious* of him behind her.

'And don't think you can arouse me by using Italian words, either,' she tossed over her shoulder. She turned to reinforce the command with a glare and noticed a dark gleam in his eyes, but it might have been a trick of the sunlight.

With chillingly elaborate courtesy he opened the car door for her. Before she got in, in a last—ditch effort to calm things down, she paused. She drew a long deep breath.

'Look, Valentino…'

His eyes glinted. *'Sì?'*

'*If* for some reason you mistakenly thought…'

'I thought *nothing*. You have every right to say no.' There was a pride and dignity in his bearing that touched her, and she was so relieved to find him civilised and accepting of her rejection, she almost felt a rush of warmth towards him.

'Oh, look. Thank you for being so...' Her words dried up and she gestured instead.

He shrugged. 'Forget it. *Una bella ragazza ha il diritto cambiare pensiero.*'

She had no idea what that meant, only that it slid down her spine like honey. But she could hardly beg him to stop breaking into his own language, especially in an emotional situation where it was only natural that it should spring first to his tongue.

The journey into Positano was short, thank the Lord, with Valentino grimly polite. That didn't succeed in alleviating the undercurrents smouldering between them. With almost punishing kindness he pointed out things to her as they drove the single road that snaked back and forth in its descent through the town to the sea. He showed her the main square, the market and the shops crammed along intriguing little alleyways, in the most courteous voice imaginable, while, confusingly, his accent deepened and became even more appealing to the ear.

It was torture.

Even worse than the aftermath of the kiss, if possible, was her awareness of the exhibition she'd made of herself during the journey, freezing with fear like that in the car. Her delight in her first sight of the amazing old village cascading down the cliff, the terraces and villas built seemingly on top of one another, was all but ruined.

He drove her almost down as far as the sea, drawing up in a small square before the small church. Taking her bags from the car, he carried them up through a maze of narrow alleyways that here and there turned into steep stairs hewn from the rock face. Eventually he pushed open a gate that led into a terrace with a little courtyard.

There were several apartments of pale pink stucco in the

row, each with a balcony under an arcaded roof. Pia followed the apartment numbers with her eye and found Lauren's at the end. She hoisted the canvas bag onto her shoulder while Valentino hefted her suitcase upstairs to the balcony.

'Do you have a key?' he said, pausing.

'Above the mantel, Lauren said.' Constraint made her voice sound unnatural even to her own ears. She reached up to the beam but he was there before her, his cool hand colliding with hers on the ledge.

She drew hers sharply away.

He gave her the key and she unlocked and stood aside for him to carry in her things. She barely noticed the apartment's interior, she was so intensely aware of Valentino and the brooding vibrations.

When her stuff was inside and he was outside on the balcony, ready to depart, she racked her brains for something to say to ease the strained atmosphere.

'Where did you say you live?' she enquired, in too much dismay to give the miraculous houses, apartment blocks and tiny terraced gardens crammed on the hillside above and adjacent to Lauren's terrace more than a cursory glance.

'There.' He pointed below.

Her eyes jolted wide open. The dwelling he indicated was nearby, all right. It was on the next level down, an elegant white villa with a broad terrace at the rear and a small, cultivated garden, with grape vines, peach and lemon trees. Set into the terrace, an irregularly shaped pool sparkled in the midday sun like a jewel, and beyond the villa was the sea.

'Oh,' she exclaimed, swallowing, 'I hadn't realised you would be so—close.'

His eyes veiled and he turned away, muttering with grim courtesy, 'Not too close, I hope.'

She lowered her gaze and edged back into her doorway. It was hard to know what to say, faced by all that spectacular beauty and a smouldering Italiano.

'Well... Thank you for—everything.' She scrabbled in her purse for some notes. 'I hope you will allow me to contribute to the petrol.'

He stiffened his wide shoulders and waved away her proffered euros. 'Please. We are neighbours. In Positano neighbours open their hearts and their generosity.'

She flushed, feeling as if her offer had contravened some unspoken tenet of gracious behaviour.

He made a move towards the steps, then halted and turned to her. His dark eyes flickered over her, measuring, assessing. 'Tell me. Have you always been so afraid of men?'

She gasped. 'I am not *afraid* of—*anything*. Far from it. I am as *open* to...as—as comfortable with...I—I *enjoy*...'

As she stuttered her denials he tilted his dark head to one side and his expression grew gravely sympathetic, and she realised she was protesting too much.

At once she checked the flow and, lifting a haughty eyebrow, gathered her womanly poise around her. 'I just prefer to feel some attraction to the man I'm kissing.'

With a cool, rather cruel smile she stepped back inside and closed the door in his face.

CHAPTER FOUR

FROWNING like a thundercloud, Valentino pushed open the black wrought-iron gate and strode beneath his grandfather's grape arbour to the side entrance, dropping his suitcase and brief-case while he searched his pockets for the key.

There was a jagged lump in his chest. Far from improving, his mood had worsened. His heart felt too heavy for him to talk to Nonno just yet. There were issues he needed to think through.

Women.

If Nonno saw him like this… In a bid to collect his cool before he worried the old guy unnecessarily, he strolled around to the pool terrace and surveyed the garden. Inevitably he glanced up at the neighbouring terrace.

Pia Renfern was a liar. That stuff about not feeling the attraction was rubbish, and if she hadn't been such a volatile, unpredictable, *difficult* female he'd have enjoyed proving it to her, over and over again, hot, hard and convincing.

Anyone would have thought he was a criminal. Anyone would have thought…

A guilty pang sliced him. Be honest with himself, he shouldn't have kissed her. But he was hardly made of stone, *perdio.* Of course he'd wanted to comfort her. What red-blooded man could have resisted when she was looking so pale and vulnerable, standing on that cliff pretending with all her heart to be brave?

And it wasn't as if she hadn't been fluttering her lashes at him. The messages there had been plain for any man to read.

Still, he had to acknowledge he'd let himself down. He'd betrayed his calling and the unspoken trust he'd painstakingly built with her on the journey, and it ate at him that a woman, *any* woman, should have such a low opinion of him. Ariana, naturally enough, thought he was a bastard of the first water for all the times he'd neglected her and put his work first, and, sure, he was guilty as charged and had paid the price. *What* a price. His guts clenched to think of it. But even she, with all the things she'd said spurred on by that vixen she called her friend, had never had any reason to condemn him like *this*.

To think that he, Valentino Silvestri, CIO and consultant to twenty-seven national police forces, was accused of being some low slimy sleaze who'd *take advantage...*

Even thinking the words pierced his guts like a hot skewer. The sense of shame jabbing him every time he thought of the momentary fear he'd glimpsed in Pia Renfern's blue eyes swelled until it inhabited his whole being. He clenched his fist and punched the wall. He shouldn't have touched a hair of her head, though, *sacramento*, it was only a kiss, and tame at that. Who'd have guessed she'd have turned into such a fiery little virago?

If only she could have put aside all her womanly rules and reservations and just... He closed his eyes, reliving those delicious initial moments when her soft curves had melted against him and he'd felt the thrill surge through their entwined bodies. There was passion in her. She'd felt the desire, all right. Every fibre of instinct and experience told him she'd felt it.

Despite himself, his incorrigible blood stirred as an intriguing thought came to him. If the desire was there burning like a low flame in her slim body, surely it was only a matter of unlocking it?

He sighed and turned back to the entrance. Forget it. She was trouble. Already he'd gone a step too far with her. He didn't *want* to see into the woman behind the face. Experience had taught him that to understand too much about what was going on inside a woman's head was the Appian Way to emotional involvement.

To know was to care. Next thing a man knew he was being measured for a wedding suit and paraded in front of the relatives like a prize bull.

Why couldn't he be like other guys he knew and feel attracted to uncomplicated women who could accept an honest attraction for what it was and were only too willing to indulge in some sweet *amore* without all the palaver?

He let himself into the villa. 'Nonno,' he called *'Dove sei?'*

After a minute the old man appeared from the direction of the kitchen. His face wreathed in smiles, and his arms opened wide.

'Tino, Tino my boy. At last. Welcome, *ragazzo*, welcome home, you young devil. Three years it's been. What kept you?'

Valentino laughed and hugged him through a wall of remorse. Was it truly three? Nonno seemed to have shrunk, and though his eyes were bright the cherished elderly frame felt more frail than he remembered.

He held the precious old vessel to him a moment longer. 'I only just found out I could come. Please—don't get too excited, Nonno. I may not be able to stay more than a few days.'

However he took that, Nonno didn't stop grinning, though his eyes grew moist.

'No matter. It's just so good for an old fool to know you bother to come to see him once in a while. Here, sit, sit down,' he exclaimed. 'You need a drink.' He handed Valentino the beer to take care of while he set about producing the cheese, the loaf, the olives and tomatoes picked from his very own garden. 'How was your trip? Did you drive all the way from France? What was the weather like there? What do you find to eat in that hellhole?'

He gave Valentino little opportunity to answer any of his

thousand and one questions, bustling about setting food on the table with spritely excitement, at the same time as hopping from one news item to the next like a mountain goat from crag to rocky crag.

'Wait until I tell you about Mirella's grandson,' Nonno crowed. 'And remember Lorenzo Corelli's sister-in-law? You'll never guess what they're saying in the *piazza*.'

Valentino lent an ear to Nonno's updates on the local gossip, knowing he'd once been the main topic of the town himself, or at least his lovely young bride had been. While he'd been involved in an undercover operation in the north, Ariana had revived an old friendship with some film people on Capri who had encouraged her to dream of a movie career.

The outcome had been inevitable. Ariana's face now smiled from the silver screen, though no longer from the pillow adjacent to Valentino's. Constant separations and the changes in Ariana, especially some illegal lifestyle choices that had outraged him when he'd found out, had damaged their relationship beyond repair. Valentino had spent too much of his professional life fighting the narcotics trade to condone his own wife's participation in some of the indulgences of her sophisticated friends.

For the first time in his life, the sordid sleeve of crime had brushed his own family. Perhaps the casual, unthinking crime of the seriously rich, but squalid nonetheless. And it seemed the languid, hedonistic friends who had seduced his bride into their glitzy world were untouchable. His burning desire to cut them to ribbons with the flaming sword of the law was frustrated.

To his eternal shame and chagrin, for the first time in his career he had a conflict of interest.

The rest was history, though he preferred not to recall the details. The painful time was something of a blur now.

Separation. Scandal. Ariana's rumoured affair with the Argentinian director. Her inability to deny it. More scandal, paparazzi dogging his footsteps for a soundbite. And as night followed day, public dishonour. Divorce, shame and an abysmal, lasting emptiness.

He shuddered. Never again. Not even a certified angel from heaven would tempt him down that thorny road again. Lucky for him Interpol had the most efficient and far-reaching database on individuals on the planet.

If by some extremely unlikely conjunction of the stars he ever reached that dangerous crossroads again with a woman, it was comforting to know he wouldn't be forced to take her on trust. If the worst came to the worst, he could run her ID through the system. Though of course, if it ever came to the point where he needed to do that, he'd know he was sick and it would be time to leave town.

'…have you, Tino?'

He started as he realised his grandfather was telling him something about the night's entertainment in the *piazza*.

'Sorry, Nonno. What was that?'

'A nice young woman,' Nonno repeated patiently. 'Some *bella ragazza* to sweeten your pillow and free you from cooking. Don't you think it's time to start afresh?'

Valentino made a rueful grimace. If only it were so simple. Nonno wasn't suggesting any modern solution to his singularity. He was talking of brides, while Valentino's preference was for less permanent arrangements. Purely physical meetings on neutral ground. No promises. No guilt attached. Honour *intacta*.

Usually.

The weight in his chest nagged and he realised what was wrong with him. If only he could think of a way to absolve his honour with Pia Renfern.

Catching sight of Nonno's lined old face puckered in anxiety, he realised he was frowning. He made the effort to summon a grin.

'I don't mind cooking, Nonno,' he said. 'It gives me a chance to think.' He clapped the old fellow on the shoulder, though not too vigorously for fear of damaging the ancient edifice. 'Now what are we doing for dinner, old man? I'm in the mood for creating a sauce.'

On her first foray out to find food, Pia was so enchanted by the long narrow staircases, the pretty lanes and gelato coloured villas overhung with purple bougainvillea, for a time she almost managed to thrust Valentino Silvestri's accusation out of her mind.

Almost.

The truth was, beneath her anger and sense of insult was the nagging knowledge that, despite her brave new face, she'd managed to expose her weakest points to the first person she met in Italy. She felt as if all her progress over the recent months, her strong and positive self-talk and courage in organising the trip, boarding the plane and flying across the world, amounted to zilch. Whether from fatigue, jet lag, or her instant and ridiculous attraction to him, she'd allowed herself to momentarily regress to her cowardly old state and Valentino Silvestri had seen straight through her.

It was so unfair.

The first attractive man in ages and with the smallest amount of stress she'd gone into instant meltdown, and in the worst and most revealing way.

If she never saw V Silvestri again it would be too soon.

At least, though, so far as everyone else in Positano knew, her slate was clean. So far. It was good that the town was abuzz with tourists. She hardly stood out as a stranger. In fact, she gloried in the anonymity. No one here was expecting her to paint, and, if she just forgot about work and enjoyed her time here, chances were it would recover itself naturally.

If she could put aside her worries about her lapse on the journey, it wasn't too optimistic to think she'd be able to start painting again soon. Wherever she looked she saw scenes begging to be brought to life on canvas.

She thought often of that moment in the car when her fingers had been itching to draw. That had been so encouraging. So like her old self. A huge energising surge of hope gathered in her. Perhaps her creativity was on the way back already.

She found the market and a greengrocer's and bought some food essentials. By that time of day there wasn't a lot of bread left to choose from in the bakery, but they managed a couple of crusty panini for her.

She climbed the steps back to Lauren's, and enjoyed stocking the fridge and making it feel like her own.

The apartment was simple and chic, and so Lauren. It was old and high-ceilinged, with blue and lemon patterned floor tiles, an airy bedroom and a sitting room lined with books and furnished with lamps, rugs, two wing chairs and a deep comfy sofa. Several of Lauren's photographic studies were hanging there, and she'd covered an entire wall with pictures of herself and her friends. Lauren had always been a great socialiser.

She'd never been the slightest bit afraid of anyone or anything.

Not that Pia *was* afraid. A little uncomfortable with heights still, perhaps, but as for being afraid of men, per se…

She drew a long simmering breath. That was simply not true. She knew what Valentino had been insinuating. 'Afraid of men' in his terms meant being afraid of *sex*.

The very idea was laughable. She'd had boyfriends, she'd had a genuine serious relationship, although she could admit now Euan hadn't been as fantastic a lover as he'd started out. Even before the bank incident he'd often rushed her and been quite insensitive. When she'd reached the point of not finding herself able to respond, he'd insinuated the fault was hers.

One good thing about that kiss this morning was the discovery that she *could* still respond. As kisses went it had been very stirring. Wasn't that why she'd called a halt to it?

Now, ironically, she was finding it hard not to dwell on it. Though so brief, the astounding power of it seemed to have sunk into her senses and stayed there. That was probably why Valentino had struck such a chord with her when he'd said he could still feel her through to his bones. In a strange way she was similarly affected, seemingly haunted by the feel of him. His taste. His quite overwhelming masculine aura.

She was sure he'd only accused her of being afraid of men to excuse his guilt and the insult to his ego. She felt perfectly justified in the things she'd said to him. Any woman would have reacted the way she had.

It was just disappointing that such an attractive man, an intelligent, charming man with that appealing accent, should have tried to turn the situation around to blame her. Certainly he could kiss well, but that was all he had going for him. Well, apart from his looks and his shoulders. All right, his eyebrows, perhaps. His hands.

In spite of his typically macho behaviour, though, her decision to search for a less physically outstanding specimen, a humble man with honour and sincerity, was in danger of sagging. She needed to remind herself of what she would have to gain from such a tranquil relationship. Who knew that she might not even meet him here in Positano? The possibility had crossed her mind once or twice before she left home.

Finding a soulmate in Italy. Perhaps like her he'd be passing through. A sensitive art curator, or some gentle billionaire who understood women, was good at expressing his feelings, and could kiss like...well, like, for example, Valentino. Someone who would understand that for her the art must always come first.

She was engaged in hanging her things in Lauren's wardrobe when she started at the sound of the doorbell. Instantly Valentino's image flashed into her head. It had to be him. Who else did she know here?

Her stomach clenched with suspense. What could he

possibly want *now*? More insults about her courage? More justifications for falling upon her like a ravenous wolf?

She checked her appearance in Lauren's large oval mirror, conscious of the sudden dryness of her mouth. To her critical eye her clothes suited her well enough. While the skirt was short, it seemed right for her legs.

At the door she hesitated, wondering if she should try to get away with pretending she was out. But then she'd never know what it was he wanted.

Screwing herself up to it, she opened the door. 'Yes?'

Though she'd expected him, the sight of Valentino in the flesh when she'd just been brooding about him seared through her like a lightning bolt. He looked taller. Straighter, somehow, and grimmer than he'd been earlier. Though he'd clearly showered and changed into lighter clothes, including a tee shirt that stretched across his powerful chest and revealed the gorgeous muscles in his arms and shoulders, she could well imagine him in a stiff white naval uniform, striding the deck of some military vessel.

His flaring dark gaze drank in the totality of her from head to toe, not missing the expanse of thigh enhanced by her skirt.

Against all the odds her pulse ratcheted up into a tribal drum tattoo.

He inclined his head and said formally, 'I am sorry to disturb you.' His eyes, shimmering with a thousand light points, captured hers and held her in mesmerised suspension. 'I have come… There is something I…' He gestured with both hands as if the words were costing him a great effort. For a guy with such athletic grace his movements seemed to acquire a surprising jerkiness. 'I—wish to apologise.'

She was stunned. 'What?'

His jaw hardened, and she noticed sinews tauten in his strong, bronzed neck. Then he said, 'I have been—considering the things you said. I accept there was no excuse for me to kiss you. I was—wrong.'

Hardly able to believe her ears in this brand new parallel universe where a man could admit a mistake, she waited for the crunch line. Surely there would be some shot at her modesty or her intelligence, courage or *something*.

But he said nothing more, just waited, his gaze on her face in burning expectation.

Called upon to respond, she dragged her brain into gear and said stiffly, 'Oh. Oh, well, then. In that case I—accept your apology. I've no doubt you probably—regret your highly inappropriate action.'

'Regret?' One black brow elevated. A glint lit his eyes, and with his hands in accompaniment he delivered a smooth flow of musical, dark chocolate Italiano that sounded to her ears almost like a denial of any regret, though it thrilled the nerve endings along her spine like a lean, caressing fingertip.

'Sorry?' she said, breathlessly reminded of how she'd felt during the kiss. How stirred up and aroused. 'I'm afraid my Italian is quite limited. What was that you said?'

He made a gesture, and his heavy black lashes descended a little. 'Only that—I regret if I caused you distress, Pia. I am not a *carogna*—a—a skunk. I am very well aware that just because a woman is beautiful and smells like a spring meadow this is not a good enough reason for a man to take her in his arms and kiss her.'

'Oh.' Shaken, while at the same time gratified that he could admit to seeing her point of view, she couldn't deny the words were intensely warming. Her lips dried even further, if possible, as the initial moments of the kiss welled up in her memory. Resisting a desire to ask him to repeat the words in the original Italian, she confined herself to, 'Fine. Good, then.'

'Even if her mouth should taste like wine.'

Those words speared through her like sparks from a meteor, but Valentino Silvestri didn't wait for her scattered wits to assemble a reply.

For an instant his dark gaze, smouldering and intense,

singed her face, lingering on her lips, then he raised his hand in a curt farewell, strode down the steps and across the court-yard to the gate.

She turned back inside in a giddy haze of relief, her heart madly thudding. Thank God for that. She could have danced at having the unpleasantness cancelled. Her spirits felt lighter, the way ahead easier. It would have been ghastly to start out in a strange town with an enemy as her neighbour. At least now she could nod to him in the street, or say hello.

She grinned to think of his flowery assertion that her lips tasted like wine. The guy must have been one of those silver-tongued Neapolitans, though, strangely, the minute she articu-lated the thought it made her heart pang. She had no desire to laugh at him, not really.

What surprised her, even moved her if the truth be told, was his sincerity. She had the feeling he'd been genuinely upset by her anger. She had to admit that for some reason, perhaps be-cause he was so good-looking, she'd made the unfair assump-tion he was a heartless operator.

She could overrule that idea now. The fact that he'd apolo-gised showed he was a man of principle.

She couldn't help wondering what it would be like to really kiss him. Earnestly, soul to soul. To be loved by someone like him. At least she knew now there was absolutely no reason to fear him. That instant of panic she'd experienced at the look-out had been unnecessary, though she couldn't have known it at the time.

She was so glad she knew it now. If she was ever offered another chance, another bite at the cherry, so to speak, maybe she wouldn't reject it out of hand. She might even embrace the moment.

CHAPTER FIVE

PIA took her omelette and salad to the balcony so she could enjoy the twilight. As the darkness gathered, the lights flickering on in the village around her brought a lump to her throat, it was so beautiful.

People were strolling by on their way to dinner or entertainments. She could hear voices of passers-by in the lane, occasional laughter. Soon music floated on the breeze. Somewhere a band was playing.

She wondered how Valentino was spending his evening. The villa below was lit like a birthday cake, as though in welcome of a beloved son. Would he have a bunch of old friends around to drink and carouse and watch football as Euan used to? Or would he have some special girlfriend, some lovely Italian woman who was only too glad to receive him back into her arms?

Somehow she didn't enjoy imagining it.

After she finished clearing away her dinner dishes she was at a loose end. Despite her long, eventful day, she was too churned up to think of going to bed. Rather than diminishing, the noise and excitement in the streets only increased. With a sudden longing to be included in the excitement, she decided to walk down to the square to see what was happening. Lauren had described Positano as the safest town in the world, and, with so many tourists to choose from, how likely was a serial killer to fasten on Pia Renfern?

She changed into her cornflower silk dress with the straps, wrapped a pashmina about her shoulders, took a torch from the kitchen shelf and walked through the gate. She'd only taken a couple of steps down when a throng of people joined in behind her. It was too late then to lose her nerve and turn tail for home. She had no choice but to allow herself to be swept along with them and continue down the steep narrow lanes towards the music.

When she reached the square she felt as if she'd walked into a party. The *piazza* was brightly lit, thronging with people and pulsing with excitement. Across from the church, a stage had been set up and a Cuban band was performing, pounding out a big professional sound. In front of it an energetic crowd of young people danced to the compulsive rhythm. The music was so infectious, even at the end of her long day Pia felt the rhythm tug at her feet.

She'd only been watching on the sidelines for a minute when a big blond Scandinavian man startled her by grabbing her arms and trying to draw her into the dance.

'No, thanks,' she said, attempting to pull away. But the guy only tightened his grip on her, inciting a blaze of anger in her.

'No,' she said fiercely, disentangling herself and glaring at him.

The guy flicked back his hair and made some huffy remark, then strode off, flexing his shoulders in offence.

Shaken, her hackles still prickling, she glanced about for a refuge and spotted an empty table at a nearby café. Quickly she threaded a path through the patrons to seize it before someone else did. She was a little surprised to notice she was clenching the torch rather firmly in her fist. The guy was luckier than he knew.

A waiter appeared and she ordered a gelato, then let her pashmina slide and sat on the edge of her chair, listening to the singer and watching the dancers. From time to time glitzy-looking couples strolled along the jetty from luxury yachts and cruisers bobbing at the pier, though she saw no movie stars or anyone she recognised as famous.

The big Scandinavian had thrown himself into salsaing with another woman now, grinning hugely and looking happy. She congratulated herself for her robust self-defence. Even so, while she felt safe sitting there in the light with the crowd thronging around her, after the guy grabbing her like that she started to feel this ridiculous dread of climbing back up those stairs in the dark.

It was insane, she knew, and she tried to reason herself out of it. Why would a murderer lurk on the steps when it would be much easier to break into her apartment and wait for her up there? Or better still, wait until later when everyone was asleep, and *then* break in?

The gelato came. It was a glorious swirl of passionfruit and vanilla, and so delicious she might have swooned with every spoonful if she didn't have that tiny lurking anxiety gnawing at her entrails.

Suddenly she sensed someone watching her. She turned to look and her lungs caught. Valentino was leaning against the wall at the entrance to one of the alleys, scanning the action, his eyes flicking through the crowd with a brooding alertness, his athletic frame devastatingly clad in black jeans and tee shirt.

He glanced across at her, then immediately looked away. That glance pierced her. Even from this distance she thought she'd seen the glint in his dark eyes. Was he pretending now he hadn't seen her? She turned her face coolly away. He was hardly likely to come over to her, was he? He'd learned he had to tread warily with her or she'd explode in his face like a fire-cracker.

The next time she glanced from the corner of her eye, he was gone.

In spite of herself she felt a pang of disappointment. At least he was someone she knew. Someone she could have talked to. After he'd taken the trouble to apologise, she'd taken it for granted that next time they met they could perhaps start again. Converse like friends.

Platonic friends, of course. He certainly wouldn't want to risk kissing her again.

Valentino started for home. A war was raging inside him. His head told him to walk away and leave well alone, while another part, a primitive, visceral region composed mainly of lust, regret and temptation, made his feet leaden and unwilling.

And there was something else. Either because of the warm evening, the excitement in the crowd or seeing her sitting there all alone like a peach ripe for the plucking, that brave little smile curling up her lips, his senses felt attuned to something elemental in the night air. It reminded him of the instant of his first sighting of her. His blood was astir, pricking as if he was on the brink of something dangerous. Dangerous, almost fateful, but...

So infinitely desirable.

The further he walked, the stronger the pull tugging him back.

Discipline was what was needed here. There were plenty of young lovelies in the town open to the possibilities of adventure. The bars were doing a roaring trade. He wouldn't have far to seek. Buy a woman a drink, say something friendly, suggest a dance...

His feet slowed to a halt.

Pia pushed her gelato aside. There was nothing for her here. No one. She might as well go home and get some sleep. Up those cut-throat stairs. She was just steeling herself to brave the murderers lining up with their knives, when the chair opposite hers was drawn back.

'*Posso?*'

She turned quickly. Valentino was gazing appraisingly down at her, desire in his eyes, the hint of a smile on his mouth. A mouth she believed now could very well have been carved by angels, having tasted it.

Her heart clocked fourteen on the Richter. '*Sì*. I mean, I mean *yes*. Yes, of course.' Her own smile broke free before she could restrain it. 'What—what are you doing here?'

He combed the throng with his dark gaze, then glanced back at her, his eyes twinkling. 'Studying the effects of starlight on the tourist population.'

It seemed to her swirling imagination the starlight was trapped inside his eyes.

'Oh, really?' she managed to say. 'What effects do you expect?'

His sensational brows twitched. 'I think there will be much—*amore*.' He smiled and her insides plunged into chaos.

She knew it was illogical to be so affected. It was no doubt that she felt thrilled and relieved to have someone to talk to in that crowd, someone she now believed she could trust. The fact that his black tee deepened his eyes to midnight satin and was filled with ravishing muscles in perfect proportion to his lean build was beside the point.

And if something pulsed between them, a current, a tension, that magnified every nuance into significance, it was the natural outcome of the day's events.

He sat down and she felt her throat sustain a delicate burn as his appreciative gaze scorched down to the neckline of her dress. The aura of subdued energy emanated from him like a silent hum of electricity.

'Am I forgiven?' He put on a contrite expression.

She lowered her lashes. 'I might come round to it.'

His eyes were amused, warm. 'So stern.'

'I can be sterner.'

Though if he only knew, her insides were in a riotous turmoil. He watched her, his mouth grave, the candlelight lending golden glimmers to his eyes.

'You are right to be severe. I was thoughtless. Can I buy you a glass of something? Wine? Espresso?'

She hesitated. 'Thank you. Wine would be nice.'

'Va bene.' He lifted an eyebrow and the waiter hastened over. After murmuring a few words to the boy, Valentino leaned back in his chair.

'You didn't care to dance with your Swedish admirer?'

'I wasn't in the mood.'

'Ah, of course. You prefer to be consulted.'

She risked a clash with the searing gaze caressing her face. 'You're learning.'

The corners of his mouth edged up and his sensual glance drifted to her throat. He said softly, 'In the case of learning, motivation is everything.'

Her heart skipped. What motivation?

He didn't explain, and she felt her blood start to course. There was nothing platonic about this conversation. Nothing at all. Desire was infecting the air like a fever, and she wasn't sure how far she wanted to be swept along with it.

The wine was set before them and he raised his glass. 'Chin chin.'

As she prepared to clink he lifted an admonishing finger to forestall her. 'Try again. When you say the words you must look into the eyes of the person. Deeply. Into the soul, now. Ready?'

Into the soul wasn't so easy. In fact, it was lethal. It could cut off someone's oxygen supply. Held breathless in his dark disturbing gaze, she repeated the words. Some words, at least.

'Chin chin chin chin chin,' he said softly, his eyes warm, caressing. As the long glance continued a flame licked her insides. 'You are *bella* in your sapphire dress.'

Her cheeks grew warm. 'Thank you. I hope you—remember what I said, though.'

His black lashes swept down. 'Sure. You don't want me to kiss you. And you don't want me to touch you.' With his sensual gaze gently mocking her, the tiny smile tickling the corners of his mouth, she wasn't so sure. Had she really said that? Had she meant it for all time? 'Is it okay if I talk to you?'

'Of course. Course it is.'

'Ah. *Grazie a Dio. Provo ricordarmi di non fare l'amore con te.*'

Maybe she should have stopped him from breaking into his seductive Italiano, but she couldn't keep making all these rules for him to adhere to. It was hardly his fault everything he said affected her like a nuclear-charged aphrodisiac. But it was flattering to feel such electric attention concentrated on her.

She risked meeting his gaze, though fleetingly. 'What was that you said?'

He spread his hands, a smile shimmering in his dark eyes. 'I forget now. How can I remember when my heart races to look at you? Maybe I was asking is it okay if I dance with you.'

His *heart* raced? Hers swelled so much it nearly exploded. If Euan had ever said anything like that...

Melting to the high-voltage persuasion, she looked at the writhing crowd of enthusiastic dancers. Some of them were fast, slick and professional, though others were at about her own moderate standard. But it was clear they were all possessed by the music, grinding their flirty hips to that very sexy beat. Except for a few adventurous cases, the action was intimate, but not so much in the touching, as in the *suggestion* of the touching.

Here was an invitation no woman could be expected to resist. Did she really want to cower on the sidelines of life for ever?

Valentino reached across and took her hand, his dark eyes aglow. *'Per favore.'*

She rose and allowed him to lead her to the dance, her heart thudding in her chest. In the midst of the crowd she faced him a breathless second. He took her hands in his strong warm grip and they began to move with tentative steps, then as their bodies grew accustomed and the hypnotic Havana beat charged her veins he pulled her closer, his hand on her ribs.

Clearly he'd done this before. He guided her a little at first, then as she grew more confident the sensual suggestion in the action of his lean hips infected her, and she forgot her inhibitions and followed his sexy lead, swinging her own hips in invitation, her skirt swirling provocatively whenever he swung her around.

Suddenly he swivelled her about and pulled her derriere hard against him, so their hips rocked in erotic unison to the seductive beat. It was so flagrantly sexual she could hardly believe it was happening. Then just when her blood was madly coursing to sensitive points north and south, he switched her around again with such effortless ease she didn't miss a step. This time he thrust his hips against hers and danced her so they rocked as one.

Dancing, held in his dark molten gaze with his hard, angular pelvis so intimately pressed against hers was so suggestive, so erotic, she felt giddy.

Giddy and aroused.

The song ended just in time and Valentino released her. The band members bowed to the enthusiastic crowd and lowered their instruments. Breathless from the exercise, her blood whipped into a fever, she joined in the applause, avoiding Valentino's eyes, and walked back to the table with him, only too conscious of his body beside hers, the occasional electric graze of his arm on her highly sensitive skin. A few people, locals she guessed, called out to him with friendly good humour, and she saw a guy nudge his neighbour, checking her out.

It was surreal. Her first day here and already she was in the company of a man, allowing herself to be carried along by events threatening to escalate out of control.

It was time—and it pained her to acknowledge it—to call

a halt. It was all too easy to be enchanted on a lovely evening when stars were shining. Sure, she'd contemplated the possibility of embracing the moment if it should arise again, but before she took another step she needed to reflect. Here she went, plunging headfirst over the Iguazu Falls of life again. Things were moving too fast.

She reached for her wrap.

He shot her a searching glance. 'You don't care to stay? I think there'll be fireworks soon.'

'Oh, that's a pity, but...it's been a long day. A long *two* days. I'm really quite—exhausted. You stay and enjoy the fireworks, though. I'll probably see you another time. Thanks for the wine, and everything. Honestly, it was...great.'

'No, no. I'll walk you back.' He didn't smile, but there was a light smouldering in his eyes that made her insides tremble. Those erotic moments in the dance hummed silently between them, whispered along her nerve endings.

Whichever way she jumped, the night seemed filled with risk.

She glanced across at the steps. Higher up they looked shadowy, and higher still pitch dark, even with the street lanterns and all the noise and laughter at this level. Was that a flash she saw up there? What was it? Moonlight glancing off a blade?

Oh, why did she have to think of that?

'It's probably not necessary for you to come,' she prevaricated. 'I'm not in the least bit nervous. But all right, if you insist. That would be very—friendly.'

He lifted his shoulders. 'I'm a friendly guy.' He gestured towards the steps. *'Andiamo.'*

Conversation was rather stilted on the climb up. The truth was she felt uncertain about what might happen when they reached the apartment. The situation was fraught with possibilities.

With the evening so warm and balmy, the scent of the sea and a man half a step behind her who'd kissed her only a few hours earlier, her senses felt wired. When she opened the wrought—iron gate and walked across the courtyard with him, then up the steps to the bougainvillea—covered balcony, she was wondering what she should say. Whether to allow something to happen, or nothing?

Oh, heavens, it was the old dilemma.

She had to admit that right then, with moonlight in Valentino's dark eyes and his pitch black hair, and the intimacy engendered by the dance winding around them like a silver ribbon, she couldn't remember ever feeling so attracted to a man. Touching him would have been so easy. *Kissing* him.

If she hadn't already made such a thing happening between them an impossibility.

When they reached her door and she produced her key, she stuttered a bit. 'Well, w-well, Valentino… It's—it's been…'

He looked grave, though his eyes still had that light in them. 'I'll say *buona notte* to you, then, Pia.'

She stared at him. *Buona notte?* Just like that? No brush of her cheek, no touching of lips, of hands? Not that she was disappointed. She was of *course* heaving a mental sigh of relief, but at the same time she felt strangely loath to let him end things so abruptly. What was he thinking, stirring her up by dancing her into a state, then leaving her high and dry?

It seemed so wrong. Once he walked down those steps she'd be alone. For all she knew Lauren's apartment was crawling with serial killers, burglars at least. It wasn't all that unlikely. Thieves preyed on visitors in tourist destinations, and she was a woman on her own. Just remembering them was enough to send fear shinning down her spine.

She eyed Valentino's tall powerful frame, the satisfying hardness of his muscles. There were times when a big strong man could be comforting to have along. If he could just walk inside with her…

'Buona notte,' she said. 'Oh, look, just a moment. Sorry,

but this lock is a little stiff and I have this stupid twinge in my fingers. Would you mind...?'

He glanced keenly at her, then with a shrug accepted the key, unlocking the door and giving it a push. She'd left all the lamps ablaze, so she could see beyond the entrance to the sitting room. As far as she could ascertain, everything was just as she had left it.

But what murderer in his right mind would wait for her in the sitting room?

Valentino moved away from the door and turned for the steps down to the courtyard. 'Okay now?'

'Yes, fine, thank you. Thank you so much,' she said, standing on the threshold. She hardly dared to push her luck another time, but when the going got rough truly jumpy people acquired the necessary nerve. 'Oh, no, wait. Just one more thing before you go. I'm having a little trouble lighting the gas ring on the stove. Would you mind terribly going into the kitchen for me and putting on the kettle?'

A gleam shot into his eyes. 'The kettle?'

'Yes,' she breathed, backing against the open front door to allow him room to pass. 'If—you wouldn't mind.'

He hesitated a second, scanning her face with a speculative gaze, his thick black lashes at a quizzical half mast, then he stepped over her threshold and walked in, his body not quite brushing her as he passed. He paused in the sitting room, glancing about with interest, and moved over to look at the photos in Lauren's display. 'Is this your cousin?'

When she nodded, he studied the eye level ones more closely for a moment, frowning. 'Does she ever work?'

'Course she does. Those were probably just times she was on vacation. Or weekends. Parties aren't against the law here, are they?'

He looked sharply at her. 'Who said anything about the law?' She blinked, and he opened his hands in a friendly gesture, grinning, then tilted his head towards the kitchen. 'This way?'

'Yes. Through there.'

She waited by the front door, but there were no cries or scuffles or sounds of serial killers being wrestled to the floor. She did hear the tap being turned on and off, a kettlish chinking, then Valentino came back.

'The kettle is on,' he said gravely. 'Will that be all?'

'Yes, thank you, that's wonderful. Oh, no, look, there is just—one other small thing.'

'*Sì?*' His eyes were glittering and alert, and a faint amusement curled one corner of his sensuous mouth. 'How else can I be of assistance?'

She took a deep bracing breath, then said it as fast as she coherently could. 'Would you—if this isn't the most frightful inconvenience—*would* you mind going into the bedroom and seeing if I left my slippers under the bed? My feet are hurting after all that dancing and I have a terrible crick in my back.' Wincing, she clutched the small of her back.

He laughed, then swung around and headed for the passage that led to the bedroom. From the rear, the black jeans encased his slim, athletic buttocks to snug perfection. To the artistic eye the sight was distinctly engaging.

While he was in there he called out, 'Is there anything you would like me to get from the bathroom? Should I check the laundry for soap?'

'Don't be silly,' she mumbled. As if anyone could hide in that tiny little bathroom. Even the shower had glass walls.

He returned, the sensual light in his eyes again. 'There were no slippers I could find. And nothing under the bed except a little dust. But there was a very pretty nightdress *on* the bed.'

Why did her neck always have to burn like a beacon? 'I must have left the slippers somewhere else. I hope you don't think…'

'I think…' He moved closer to her. Very close. So close she could feel the heat from his big, lean body. Strangely, she wasn't even tempted to panic. She didn't back away, instead she had a wild longing to butterfly kiss his long lashes, just to experience them to the full. As a beginning.

'I think maybe you are feeling alone in a strange country.' His accent had thickened. 'And this reminds me of something I need to consult with you about.'

'Oh, yes?' she breathed, allowing her sultry gaze to drift to his masculine mouth. 'What would that be?'

'If I were to hold you, very gently, like this...' He placed his hands lightly on her shoulders. His voice was caressing, and so were the lean, hard hands. Before long they were sliding up and down her arms with a hypnotic motion, sending tingles through her skin. 'Would that feel—inappropriate?'

'I don't think so. I think it would feel...absolutely...' She was breathing so hard it was impossible to maintain coherence. As his gorgeous lips moved dangerously closer to hers her heart was cavorting on the edge of a vertical cliff. 'Just—just so absolutely...'

The lights went out. Or maybe it was that he kissed her.

Whatever came first, he kissed her.

Perhaps she should have complained. He wasn't obeying her embargo, and what about her fatigue? But sometimes on a starry night a failed kiss deserved a second chance, just for the sake of cosmic completion. So this time their tongues collided sexily, and in the dark she wasn't nearly as reserved as she had been the first time. Her senses recognised the taste and scent of him and opened to him like desert flowers to the rain.

And when his hot hands squeezed her breasts and he bent his mouth to each tender nipple and sucked her through the blue satin, desire rekindled in her blood and flared to a roar, and she panted, rasping in his arms like a desperate creature.

He pushed her up against the open door, devouring her face, her throat, the swells of her breasts with his lips, and all that kept her from fainting from the thrilling, mind-blowing pleasure was the delicious, wicked ache between her legs and a primitive anticipation.

His bold hands made urgent explorations of her curves. For once she adored the exciting dark. It gave her licence to encourage him and hope he might be spurred on to greater acts of boldness. He was well aroused, it was clear, and almost unconsciously her greedy hands trailed up and down the flattering bulge in his jeans.

A shudder rocked through him. He grabbed her hands and held them still, then took the most fantastic retaliation.

In a shocking, ruthless move he slid *his* hand right up her dress and stroked her most sensitive, intimate place through the flimsy cotton of her pants.

Oh, God in heaven.

He continued the exquisite caress, and waves of pleasure radiated throughout the crucial region. It was sheer bliss, it was rapture, and some dim, cautious part of her in her grandmother's voice was moaning that she shouldn't be allowing it, which was a surefire sign it was *right*. And as if the heavens were suddenly involved, the sky was all at once split with explosions of bright iridescent colour, but she was too enthralled to notice much of that. She clung to him, locked in the kiss, a prisoner of forbidden ecstasy.

At last the lights flickered on and the spell was broken. Valentino released her, then fell back, his powerful chest still rising and falling. His dark eyes were aflame.

'You are…*squisito*,' he said hoarsely, his voice thick and intense. He took her arms in his hands and drew her back towards him. But an ear-piercing shriek that might have been going on for some time finally penetrated the misty haze of her pleasure, and her addled brain synapses somehow made the connection.

Gasping, she tore herself away from him. 'Oh, that's the kettle. Sorry.'

She hurried to the kitchen, as fast as it was possible on

jellied limbs, and turned off the flame, killing the hideous noise. During all the excitement, the water had nearly boiled away. She turned away from the stove and ran her hand through her hair, smoothed down her dress with trembly hands.

Now what? Her dilemma had reached the next stage, to tell the truth. A hotly aroused man was out there in her sitting room with strong expectations. Expectations she'd done nothing to quell. *But...*

On the one hand she'd only just met him, and where could it go from here? On the other, he was gorgeous, she was free, twenty-six and in charge of her life, and she had nothing to lose except her heart.

Surely it was time to rise to the occasion, act like a woman and take the next chance?

In the sitting room, meanwhile, Valentino's veins drummed with a delicious certainty. Dangerous the temptation might be, but as irresistible as the rotation of the planets. Giving his jaw a rub to check it was still smooth, he paused by the mass of pictures on the display wall.

A shot of Capri caught his eye. He looked closer, then cast an idle glance over the rest. Pia's cousin appeared to have a wide circle of friends. People grinning from beaches, bars and restaurants, dancing, picnicking, hiking. Lauren and friends, lazing beside an exotic pool at some mountainside villa, waving from a yacht, linking arms with the same smiling elegant couple.

That couple.

The raw spot in his gut took a savage jab. He leaned closer for a better look.

Surely that was Giancarlo Fiorello and his wife. Here they were again, a different occasion with different people. And here again. Scanning more of the pictures, he thought he recognised the settings. Frequently, in fact over and over again, it was the house. The house he suspected and loathed. The Villa

Fiorello. The indoor pool, the outdoor pool, the balconies, the vines. The loggia, the roof.

The big muscle inside his chest felt squeezed in a vice. The scene of Ariana's betrayal. Her first betrayal, that was. Or at least, the first he knew about.

What was Lauren Renfern's involvement with those people?

Resistance to the jumble of ideas clamouring in his brain was uppermost at first. The cousin's friendships didn't affect anything here. Not Pia, not this occasion, not the promise of passion. But against his pleasure, against his sweet anticipation, a chill reality solidified in his mind.

Lauren Renfern…Pia Renfern. How close were the cousins? How alike?

His desire was doused as effectively as if he'd plunged into an arctic sea. Reaching, he unpinned a clear shot of Lauren and slipped it into his pocket.

Pia floated back to the sitting room on a cloud of adrenaline. Though she'd only been absent a minute or so, the instant she swanned in she sensed the atmospheric shift. Instead of seething with barely contained lust, Valentino was scanning the wall of photographs.

He turned sharply when she approached, a sharp crease between his brows. 'Ah,' he said. His eyes were glinting, but not with the flame they'd held a few moments earlier. 'How well does your cousin know these people?'

'Who? What people?' She peered closer at the photos and saw several of Lauren with a couple.

He indicated. 'Here. Giancarlo and Lola Fiorello.'

She lifted her brows in recognition of the name. 'Oh, so that's them. Lauren's quite friendly with Lola, I think. She often goes over to Capri to visit them. I think Lauren said—' She broke off. Valentino was studying her narrowly. Far from gazing upon her like a silver-tongued Neapolitan desirous of ravishing her into a state of delirium, his eyes were hooded. Distant.

She felt a pang of misgiving. 'Is something wrong?'

His black lashes lowered. 'Not at all. But I'm—afraid I have to leave you.' He made a move for the door, then half turned. 'Are you feeling safe now?'

'Safe? Of course I feel *safe*. I feel perfectly *safe*.'

He made a slight twitch of his lip at her assertions. *'Bene.'*

As if safety were the issue *now*. She was in a romantic state. And psyched up to face the moment of truth, her blood pumping in a fever of nervous anticipation and hope. But to her astonishment, after a hesitant instant in which he moved towards her and she half thought he was about to take her in his arms, he restricted himself to lifting his hand in a curt farewell gesture, then strode swiftly to the door.

'We'll talk tomorrow,' he said, and was gone.

Gone.

Valentino walked soundlessly across the tiles and up the stairs. He paused for a moment at his grandfather's door and listened to the steady rhythm of his breathing.

In his study, the scanner groaned when he switched it on, the lights flashing before settling to green. It took him no time to send Lauren Renfern's photo to his night staff in Lyon with a priority request attached. It would be daylight in the Antipodes, a good time to scan the Australian national databases.

Birth and death records, police and military files, passport, education, health, bank and credit histories were only a start. Interpol's connections could unearth almost every transaction an individual had ever participated in. And that was even before mining the bounty of information left by their Internet social footprint. If Lauren Renfern was involved in anything illegal with the Fiorellos, if she'd only just *thought* about it, his team would find it. And if Pia Renfern had come here to join them, he would…

What?

Prevent her, or catch her?

He felt a nasty twinge in his bones. Did he really need to check up on her? What if the cousin was a cleanskin? Couldn't he just enjoy the rapport he'd established with Pia and let it unfold?

A little romance, some physical pleasure. Days in the sun. Nights… A mild degree of intimacy, laughter. He hated the thought of checking on a woman's background. A potential lover. Wouldn't it feel like a betrayal?

If he thought about it, he realised she hadn't told him much about herself. But then, who did when they met someone for the first time? *Sacramento*, this time it suited his purpose. He didn't *want* to know too much, did he?

This was his way. Keep things light. Only talk about the present. Don't let the past intrude.

The temptation to let his misgivings slide and take her to his bed regardless overwhelmed him for several moments, but with a grim wrench he reminded himself of who and what he was.

Better to settle any queries now before he got in any deeper.

The irony of his position didn't escape him. The risk of knowing more about her was equal to the risk of knowing nothing at all. On the one hand he had a burning desire to know everything, on the other a desperate need *not* to. What, *perdio*, was wrong with him? He must have been too long without a woman.

While there was even the slightest doubt he mustn't get too close to her. If she was dishonest, integrity demanded he should have no compunction about alerting the *carabinieri* and seeing her behind bars. Surely.

Like an old refrain the words *conflict of interest* began to rumble in the back of his brain. Never again must he risk allowing history to repeat itself, though maybe he'd wait, at least until he had a photo of her.

He moved to the window and parted the blinds. The upper terrace's end apartment was in darkness. She'd gone to her bed.

He imagined her slim body prone on the sheet, her breasts pushing against the material of that gauzy nightdress he'd seen, and sighed. He could still feel their softness in his hands. He hadn't seen her naked nipples, but through her clothes he'd tasted their tautness and his imagination had been aroused more potently than if he'd enjoyed an actual sighting. The vision rose in his mind now with overwhelming immediacy. Raspberries, sweet, taut and edible.

His loins stirred and he tried to force his mind to other things. It was clear he needed to establish some objective distance. She'd looked and tasted so...sweet.

If Pia Renfern *was* the innocent she seemed someone should protect her. A tender woman in a foreign land could so easily be taken advantage of if some responsible person wasn't alert to the possibilities.

Lucky for her, he was alert.

CHAPTER SIX

PIA woke from a long deep slumber with a foggy feeling of misgiving. When her brain cleared and the previous evening flooded back, she only succeeded in feeling more and more mystified.

What had really happened? One minute she'd been believing in the magic, well on the way to a night of pure passion, the next everything had ground to a halt and there had been an abrupt goodnight.

Was she so out of practice at reading the signals? Or maybe, just maybe, she hadn't communicated her own signals very well herself. She scrolled back through the events leading up to the kiss, and then the kiss itself. Until that point Valentino's enthusiasm had been clearly apparent. Then there'd been the kettle interruption.

That had been the point when everything changed. It was as if, with her having left the room, Valentino had had time to rethink. Perhaps, following her outburst at the lookout, he'd decided not to risk going any further. Or maybe he was just being a fantastic gentleman, waiting until they knew each other better.

She screwed up her face. With what she knew of the male animal, how likely was that? No, in some way she'd slipped up. She must have taken too long in the kitchen, and he'd made the assumption she was *scared*.

Oh, *God*, no. How humiliating.

The shame of it rocked her. No wonder he'd changed the subject and started taking such a forensic interest in Lauren's wall. He was trying to spare her embarrassment by easing out of the situation. As if any man would really be diverted by a picture of some acquaintances.

She closed her eyes and breathed hard. Every exchange with Valentino Silvestri had ended badly. Somehow she would have to nip this notion he had in the bud. In fact, why even bother? The best thing she could do would be to forget him, stop reliving that kiss, not think about dancing, moonlight, or fireworks, and focus on her real reason for being here.

Determined to hold to that positive thought, she managed the transition from the bed to the bathroom. Warbling in the shower, she had the strongest inkling in ages that she was on the verge of painting, perhaps some lush landscape in rich sensuous oils. Maybe even a series.

She could feel the work building up inside her in the way things always used to. Her fingertips were practically itching to take up a brush. She sensed the moment was close. Maybe she could even start a portrait. Something insightful involving a lean, hard man with elegant, bronzed hands and bristling eyebrows.

In her impatience to start she skipped breakfast. She put on her old spattered painting shirt, took her sketchbook out to the balcony with her fingers crossed and a prayer in her heart, and faced the morning.

The world was so breathtakingly beautiful.

Overnight a large yacht had dropped anchor in the harbour. It was a long way out, but she could easily distinguish a helicopter pad at both bow and stern. Wow. Someone was rich.

She leaned over the balustrade. On the terrace below, an old man was working in the garden. Valentino's grandfather, she guessed. He was digging, though every so often he stooped to drag something from the earth.

With such a scene of contradictions begging, how could she not be inspired?

She filled a blue ceramic bowl with lemons and placed it on the balcony table. Holding her brush poised, she breathed deeply until she felt her senses fill with the essences of her surroundings. The cascading villas, the sunlit sea, the rough tiles under her feet, the heady scents of citrus, the fat vine leaves twining round the arches...

Willing the inspiration to flow, she paused to wipe a trickle of perspiration from her neck. A white flash caught the corner of her eye.

Damn. Valentino was standing on his terrace.

Her pulse jumped into a higher gear and she leaned forward for a better view through the holes in the balustrade. Oh, glory, he was wearing shorts and a singlet top, showcasing those fabulous shoulders and long bronzed thighs.

She watched him take the steps down to the terraced garden. The old man paused to greet him with a nod, wiping his brow with the back of his hand. Valentino patted him on the shoulder, and the old guy planted his shovel upright in the ground and turned away towards the house.

Pia was intrigued then to see Valentino take the shovel in hand. After a few minutes of easy, rhythmic, almost lazy digging—poetry in motion from a purely artistic point of view—she was even more intrigued to see him take off his vest and toss it over the bough of a small peach tree, then really swing into his task.

Like a dreamer Pia stared, hypnotised. A sensual warmth flooded her and she felt her hands and armpits moisten. For a few hazy seconds she was aware of her heightened pulse drumming in her ears. The undeniable beauty of his powerful shoulders, strong sinewy arms and long muscled back rippling in the sun, glistening with sweat, rushed through her blood like an intoxicant.

She slid off her chair and knelt down on the tiles for a

better view, breathing hard. Call it desire, call it madness, but Valentino Silvestri was a sight worth seeing. Why hadn't he wanted to stay? Had she unconsciously radiated the sort of neediness that had so repelled Euan?

After a while the old man came out and beckoned, and Valentino planted the shovel and went back inside. The show was over.

Tottering to her feet, she cleared away her palette and brushes. There was no way she could concentrate now.

She changed into her peasant blouse with the puffed sleeves and front lacing, a skirt and sandals, and, taking her camera, locked the apartment behind her.

Photography had often been a fruitful way to kick-start her creativity, and here in paradise there were subjects in every direction. She discovered she wasn't the only one enthralled by the beauty. Down at the beach a street artist had set up his easel and was dashing off masterpieces for the tourists. How she envied him his confident reliance on his abilities.

She watched him for a few wistful minutes. She'd love to be doing just that. Lining up the perspective with her eye, dabbling her brush or her knife, choosing the magic starting spot, slapping on the colour with sensuous abandon.

She raised her camera to the artist and digitally immortalised him, then snapped a few other great shots. Heading up from the beach she was tempted from the main road by a narrow alley, half lane, half staircase, barely wide enough for two people to pass.

Pausing to photograph some verdigris-encrusted scrollwork on an old street sign, she noticed a figure rounding the corner into the lane. Almost before her eyes registered Valentino her heart did, racketing into a fast tattoo. He advanced up the steep path towards her, his dark brows lowered in brooding contemplation.

He looked up and instantly his expression alerted, his eyes

raking over her in her skirt and pretty top with a piercing masculine interest.

'Oh. Valentino,' she said, as breathless as if she'd been running. 'Hello.' He looked crisp and freshly showered, his lean frame now clad in jeans and a white open-necked shirt that enhanced his olive tan.

Their interrupted embrace of the evening before resonated vibrantly in the air. If only there were some safe, non-revealing way to ask for an explanation.

'Pia,' he acknowledged, his thick lashes sweeping down.

'How...how are you? Is everything—all right with you?' She looked carefully at him.

'Everything is fine.'

'Both mentally and physically?'

A gleam crept into his eyes. 'All is in exceptionally good working order, you will be pleased to hear. And you? Did you sleep well? Your pillow is soft, your bed?' His thick black lashes couldn't quite conceal the sensual admiration in his eyes. If he'd found her so unattractive that he needed to bolt the evening before, he wasn't showing it now.

'Oh, yes, the pillow...and the—the bed. They're very comfortable. Soft, and at the same time quite springy. Bouncy, even, if you can imagine that,' she added with a small gurgle of a laugh.

His hot eyes darkened and she could feel the tension in him like a tangible thing. His gaze flickered to her throat, her legs. When he spoke his voice was deeper. Husky, even. 'I am imagining it.' His glance lighted on her camera. 'Are you a photographer like your cousin?'

She shook her head. 'Not me. I'm afraid I'm just an amateur.'

He held out his hand. 'Here, I'll take your picture.'

Her immediate instinct was to refuse, she rarely liked herself in photos, but she didn't like to be churlish.

'Oh.' She shrugged. 'Well, all right. That's—very kind.' She handed the camera over, careful not to touch his fingers as she showed him the trigger, then glanced about her for a backdrop. 'Er—here will do. This pink wall.'

She stood back against the wall like a firing squad victim while he raised the camera. She felt so self-conscious with his dark gaze focused directly on her, she could feel a hot flush rising. At the same time, warring with her embarrassment was another sensation creeping down her arteries. It was almost a thrill. Almost—like being aroused.

She noticed the corners of his mouth tilting up, then after a fraught second he lowered the camera. 'You need to relax a little.' His voice sounded deeper and richer somehow, almost a caress.

'I am relaxed.' She tried to lighten her expression with a phoney smile.

He tried again and snapped her this time, then inspected the result. *'Bella,'* he said softly, then moved close to show her.

She caught a flash of her silly, smiling face, but she could barely take the picture in. His bare forearm had lightly brushed hers, sending her skin cells into a frenzy while her senses went tripping in recognition of his now familiar scent.

Gravely he gave her back the camera. 'And another.'

Before she understood what he meant, he whipped out his mobile and clicked another couple of shots. He examined them with satisfaction, clicked something, then tucked his mobile away. *'Si arrosse al pensiero, Pia, non ti preoccupare. Non ho nessun intenzione di baciarti questo momento.'*

'Sorry, I'm afraid I don't…' Her lashes fluttered uncontrollably. 'What was that in English?'

'Ah.' He made an apologetic gesture. 'I was forgetting. I was saying that you are blushing like a rose.

She grew warmer, if possible. 'What else did you say? There was more, wasn't there?'

His thick lashes drifted heavily down. 'Only that you have no need to be worried, *tesoro*. I am not thinking of kissing you here. When I taste your sweet lips we must be alone together, in a private place. There are too many gossips in this village.'

Her sweet lips turned as dry as old crackers. She resisted licking them and drew in a long, trembling breath. 'You're mistaken, Valentino. I wasn't worried. But I'm surprised. I'm not sure why you sound so confident, as if you expect there to be more of…this.' She made a wordless gesture.

'This…?'

'You know. The kissing, et cetera.'

He looked amused. 'Aren't you anticipating more of the kissing? Et cetera?' His eyes were teasing, sensual.

She flushed, but said steadily, 'I advise you not to rely on it. It will depend on how I feel, don't you think?'

'It might also depend on how *I* feel,' he said, smiling. 'But let me assure you, as far as I could ascertain, you do feel simply—*fantastico.*' He softened his voice, lacing the double entendre with such lascivious meaning she nearly gasped.

Rallying, she lifted her brows. 'And yet you ran away.'

Amusement played on his sexy mouth. 'So I did. Did that matter?'

That she was left dangling in a state of arousal? She felt a spurt of indignation, but achieved a sweet smile. 'Not in the slightest. I was grateful for your consideration. Thank you for understanding how desperately tired I was. I appreciated the early night.'

'Prego.' Valentino curled his lips into the requisite answering smile. In spite of his comprehension of her pique he felt the heat of challenge surge through him.

He'd make her admit it mattered whether he stayed or went. He'd make her burn for him and beg.

'I'm glad you are well rested.' He moved close to her, took her arms and drew her into him, his blood stirring to the feel of her soft breasts and thighs, the fragrance of her hair. How things had changed in a few short hours. In spite of her defiant words she didn't demur at his touch and once again he was back on the verge of the most delicious victory.

Surely her mouth was the most enticing he'd ever laid eyes on. He bent to kiss her, intending only a light brushing of lips, but unable to draw back until his blood was racing, she was trembling and melting in his arms, her sweet breath mingling with his, her sweet nipples taut against his chest.

The sound of voices alerted Pia to people advancing towards them in the lane, and the kiss broke. At once he dropped his hands and they were separate, although in her giddy aroused state Pia felt the desire bonding them like an invisible cord.

'This afternoon,' he said thickly. 'I'll bring you some raspberries to match your—your tongue.'

Her *tongue*? Then she blinked. *This afternoon?*

'Come,' he said, catching her hand. 'Walk up to the *piazza* with me.'

Why was real life never the way it was rehearsed? Hadn't she resolved to pull the plug on him? She'd just been the easiest pushover. And what was more, judging by the gleam in Valentino's eyes, he was perfectly aware of it, *and* her reluctance to make the cut.

Oh, admit it, she was reluctant. It was so pleasant having a hot-blooded man saying passionate things to her no other man would have thought of in his wildest dreams. When had Euan ever thought of matching her tongue with raspberries? She was starting to wonder how she'd ever lived without the Italian style. From now on she would insist on it as her benchmark.

They reached the square at the top of the town. Valentino took her elbow and ushered her up a step into the open-air café. A waiter greeted him by name and showed them to a table, swiftly providing them with a carafe of water, then stood at the ready, his dark eyes flicking from one to the other of them.

'*Capuccino, per favore,*' she said. Valentino made an

amused sound and she lifted her brows at him. 'What's wrong with that?'

'Only barbarians drink cappucino so late in the day.' His eyes were warm and caressing, as if he found barbarians quite appealing.

'Do they?' She smiled at the waiter. 'Forgive me, I'm a bar-barian.'

The waiter grinned and assured her it was okay. He was used to *turisti*. Valentino intervened then to introduce them. 'Pia, meet Tony. Tony, Signorina Renfern.'

'Buongiorno,' she said, offering Tony her hand. 'Didn't I see you last night in the square?'

'Sure, I was there,' Tony exclaimed. 'And I saw you. Dancing, dancing.' He wiggled his narrow hips. 'The music was not bad, hey? Good for exercising. Did you like the fire-works?'

'Oh, the—fireworks.' She felt warmth creep up her neck. *'Yes*, they were…' She risked the briefest glance at Valentino. He was watching her face, his mouth grave, his acute dark gaze amused while at the same time veiled.

'Fantastic,' he said softly.

She looked at his hands, and the glow seeped further, up into her cheeks and ears. 'Yes. They were.' She breathed the words.

The young man whisked away and she took up the menu and fanned her face.

Valentino lounged idly back in his chair. 'There'll be more tonight.' His lean face was non-committal.

'More…?' She held the fan still.

'Fireworks.'

A bolt of pure excitement shot through her, though she man-aged to conceal it. 'Do you know that for certain, or is it just wishful thinking?'

'You could say both.' The corners of his mouth edged into

a smile that brought an extra surge of warmth to swell her breasts.

'You're very confident.'

'I am. Well, I've always had a special interest in pyro-technics.'

His eyes were mocking, sensual, and so damnably attrac-tive. Her insides were melting and churning at the same time. She wanted to, but should she give him another chance so eas-ily? How far did he intend to go this afternoon? How far did *she*?

The coffees arrived, and she closed her eyes the better to smell the chocolatey aroma, then sipped, savouring the brew.

Valentino downed his espresso in a couple of swigs. He sat relaxed, keeping a leisurely eye on the constant parade of passers-by in the street while at the same time feeling intensely aware of his companion. The temptation to reach out and touch her was extreme. Her cheek and throat were so smooth his mouth watered. His fingers itched to untie the bow at her cleav-age and release the strings. Every so often when she moved he caught a glimpse of the valley between her breasts and his blood coursed to dangerous places.

The tension he sensed in her pulled at him with an ache that was hard to distinguish from pleasure. During the long hot night, over and over he'd examined and re-examined his need to resist her, and now here he was again, lusting, allow-ing the beast inside him to dictate.

He needed to stop looking and imagining, visualising all he'd explored in the vibrant dark. If only his hands didn't re-member so well the size and shape of her breasts. So soft and resilient, so responsive...

Once more his conscience pricked him. There he went, slip-sliding again. He needed to tighten his grip on himself. From the first sight of her walking in the alley, her graceful limbs outlined by the soft fabric of her skirt, he'd wondered if he would have the strength to resist her if he uncovered something negative.

Last night's trawl through the databases had unearthed nothing especially suspicious about the cousin, apart from her frequent need to travel, and his instincts told him Pia was just exactly as she seemed. A young woman taking advantage of her cousin's invitation to enjoy a holiday on the other side of the world.

But how dependable were his instincts?

He needed to discipline himself, cut the sexy talk and use this time with her fruitfully, instead of as an opportunity to lure her a step closer to his bed.

He cooled his tone, though not so much it would alarm her. 'How long since you saw your cousin?'

As though sensing the change in temperature, she glanced at him quickly. 'Not that long. She came to Dad's funeral.'

'Ah. How recently has your father…?'

'Last year… He—he—had a heart attack.'

Picking up something in her voice, he allowed a beat to go by before he said casually, 'Were you close?'

'We were, yes.' Pia turned her face to the street but her eyes were suddenly so misty she couldn't see the view. Funny how she could feel so excited and attracted and want to cry all at the same time. But this was hardly the time for tears. Hell, if she opened those floodgates the flow would never stop. She fought them back.

For a surprised instant Valentino caught the shimmer in her eyes and something tugged in his chest. Her loss was recent, he realised, and she wasn't over it. His perceptions of her made a shift.

She was smiling again, but the glimpse of her fragility pierced him in some way.

Instantly he tried to shut down the response. *Too much information.*

'Nothing ever prepares you for the shock,' she continued.

'You think you would adapt, you've been subconsciously expecting it all your life, and then, when it finally happens you
realise a major chunk of who you are, your very foundations,
has gone, and you were never...' She raised her blue eyes to
his, their rueful appeal touching him in places that were off
limits. 'Sorry to rattle on. Anyway, you must know what it's
like. You've lost both your parents, didn't you say?'

'Sure.' He tried avoiding her gaze. Overly conscious of his
blood's rapid beating, he curled his fingers into his palms.
Sacramento, what was he doing? All he'd wanted to know
were a few facts.

He really needed to cool it. He wasn't handling this at all
well. Next thing he knew... *Mio Dio*, next thing he'd be letting
himself get attached to her.

Pia sensed his withdrawal and bit her lip. Had she said too
much? She supposed she was still quite rocky over her father.
With the bank incident happening so soon after the funeral,
she guessed she hadn't really had time to properly process all
that losing him meant before she'd taken the plunge to rock
bottom.

She drew a deep breath. This was neither the time nor the
place. She needed to stay away from the minefields. Keep the
lid firmly on.

'Hey, Valentino.'

'Oh, look,' she said, directing Valentino's gaze to the street,
relieved to be rescued from the awkward moment. 'I think he's
waving to you.'

An elderly gent dressed in a white suit and cap, colourful
shirt, wide silk tie and white leather shoes stood outside the
railing, waving his cane. Valentino sprang up, and the old man
hobbled up into the café to embrace him.

After a warm exchange of greetings Valentino introduced
him as Luigi, a great friend of his grandfather, and invited the
old boy to join them. Luigi greeted Pia with courtesy in very

halting English, then embarked on a rapid-fire conversation with Valentino in his own language.

Pia listened for a while, straining her ears for the words and phrases she knew. This was a valuable moment, she realised. Though she couldn't understand most of the words, she felt in some way included in a tiny piece of Positano life from the inside. Absently she reached into her shoulder bag and felt for a pencil and the notebook that lived there.

With Valentino's attention focused intently on his friend, she had leisure to study their faces. The older face and the younger. She drew a few swift down-strokes to grab the outlines of each, then started first on Valentino's. From hairline to cheekbone to jaw, the strong column of his neck, the bronzed triangle of his collar opening. Then she turned her attention to his brows, feathering in their richness in quick little strokes.

Her hand flew over the paper of its own accord while her hungry eyes devoured Valentino, every strong, beautiful line and hollow, every flicker of his long lashes, the line that curled up at the corner of his mouth, storing it all up for later. Storing him up.

Then she started on the old man, lines and hollows, cracks and crevices. Not a bad likeness, she judged, though necessarily crude.

The conversation came to an end and Luigi stood and took a warm leave of them both, sending a sly nod in her direction as he departed with some comment that brought a smile to Valentino's eyes, though they quickly veiled. His frown returned.

His gaze fell on her notebook. 'What's that you're doing?'

'Oh, just scribbling.' She flipped the notebook shut and slipped it into her bag. 'Luigi seemed very pleased to see you. Your grandfather must be thrilled to have you visit.'

He looked rueful. 'I've been away too long. Nonno's always been strong, as if he should go on for ever, now suddenly, when I'm not looking...' He pulled himself up, and at her querying glance his eyes veiled again. 'Forget it. It's nothing. Let's talk of what we both want to talk about.'

She lifted her brows, though her heart beat pleasantly faster. 'What might that be?'

Smiling, his gaze purposeful, he moved his chair a little closer so his hands were almost touching hers on the table. 'You and me.'

'Is there a you and me?'

Amused, he dropped his glance, then looked up, his eyes searching her face. 'Do you have an *amore*?'

'Not right now.'

His eyes were warm, though at the same time acute. He said softly, 'Allow me to guess. Someone has hurt you.'

She made a mocking tilt of her head to deflect the shrewd scrutiny of those dark eyes. 'How can you know that?'

'Why else would you be alone?'

'Why else would you?' she retorted, smiling to hide the hot flush flaring in her nape.

She leaned back in her chair and twirled her teaspoon, playing at being cool while her pulse was in training for the hurdles. One thing she wasn't about to confess was anything that had happened to her in the past year.

She added evenly, 'I'm not sure why you even want to know.'

He lifted his wide shoulders. 'I'm not sure either.' There was something in his tone, a wryness that caught at her. She looked quickly at him, but he'd lowered his black lashes, while a crease appeared between his sensational brows.

'But I want to,' he added, glancing up to look levelly at her. 'I find I must.'

She read the signs of seriousness with an alarmed lurch. Feeling the pressure, she looked away, then flashed a careful glance at him through her lashes. 'Everyone has disappointments in their life. Are you planning to tell me all of yours?'

'No. I am a gentleman.' Smiling, he scrutinised her face,

then his sensuous mouth grew grave. His lean, bronzed hand clasped hers. 'So...Pia?'

Their palms coincided and she felt the electricity of his strong masculine persona surge through her and spark some primitive, inevitable trigger. The thrilling skin to skin contact intensified, but she wasn't sure which of them increased the pressure. Only that it accelerated the excitement pulsing in her veins. She didn't draw her hand away. Couldn't.

She lifted a careless shoulder. 'It doesn't have to be a blood sport, does it? Isn't it possible people can come together for the time they find pleasure in each other, then say their good-byes with a smile and a shrug?'

He examined her face with an intent gaze. 'No promises, no pasts?'

'Why complicate things? What does the past have to do with it?'

He gazed quizzically at her. 'That sounds like a beautiful philosophy, though I would have thought...' His eyes narrowed. 'Have you always been such a free spirit? Truly?'

She hesitated. Every instinct told her this would be a mistake. A big, deadly mistake. The last thing a woman should do was to spill her guts to the most hopeful prospect of gorgeous Neapolitano machismo she was ever likely to encounter.

On the other hand, a guy was inviting her to open up. A guy with dazzling, dark eyes that could be warm and friendly, sizzling hot or impenetrable steel.

In the end, she chose her words carefully, restricting herself to saying, 'What's it all about, after all? People are attracted, then learn things about each other and—change their minds. Isn't that what you've found?'

He smiled, and this time there was ruefulness in the dark depths. 'You could say so.'

Valentino straightened a little and stretched his legs under the table. Idly he turned her hand over and studied it. While graceful it offered an impression of capability, with warm, slim fingers and nails short-trimmed, unpainted.

He signalled Tony for the bill, made small talk, discussed the passing parade of tourists, all with a sense of shock.

Here was a woman who had arrived at exactly the same conclusions he had himself. Love was best as a temporary arrangement. No past, no future, no chains.

Pia Renfern was perfect. Perfect. So why did he feel so shocked?

CHAPTER SEVEN

PIA shied away from thinking it. Once she actually allowed in such a dangerous, world-shattering thought it would transform an excited, terrified, fantastic, cliffhanging feeling into an insane reality. A reality she couldn't afford.

People who'd recently suffered a stress disorder needed to stay on an even keel. They needed order and routine. Discipline. Steadiness. They had enough trouble managing their intense emotions without falling in…

Oh, God, no. She'd nearly let it in.

She gave herself a bracing pep talk. Falling in *murk*, that was what she'd call it. Falling in murk was for dewy-eyed ingénues with dreams of wedding rings, not for artists with a goddess-granted gift they were destined to spend their lives paying homage to.

Passion was what Pia Renfern could permit herself. So long as she was lusting for Valentino Silvestri and the hairs on his forearms and his solid calves and powerful thighs she was on the most direct superhighway to perfect inner health and contentment.

Murk, on the other hand, was anti-artist. It tied a woman up in knots, soaked her in tears and wrung her to a rag. This was why, when strolling down to the *pasticceria* with Valentino, she concentrated on his right ear lobe and contemplated biting it. Anything to quell that magic, excited, enchanted, goofy, beaming, breathless sensation that kept seizing up her heart every time he turned to glance enquiringly at her, or their arms brushed.

Outside the shop they paused to taste the pastries she'd bought.

Valentino wolfed the last of his, then cast Pia a teasing look. 'What if a free spirit should decide she is missing the good things in life?'

'Things like…?'

'Status… Possessions…' He shot her a sidelong glance. His mouth edged up at the corners. *'Bambini.'*

Pia nearly choked. 'You're kidding, right? *Bambini?*'

He spread his hands. *'Sì.* You met my aunt. She is like ninety-five per cent of the women in this village. They go mad for *bambini*. They catch the virus then there's no escape. They won't rest until they have one of their own. Why should Pia Renfern be any different?'

She rose to the challenge. 'All right, then, but first things first. By status I assume you mean husband, correct?'

He shrugged and spread his hands. *'Certamente.* This is how the world works.'

She lifted a brow at that. It might indeed have been true, but to her mind it was nothing any woman, artist or no, should give the nod to.

'Well,' she said airily. 'The answer is easy. I'll achieve my own status, and be satisfied with whatever I can make of it. In the case of the *bambini*…' She dusted the icing sugar from her fingers and waggled them in the breeze. 'If I should catch the dreaded virus, I s'pose I'll be just like the others.'

'What others?'

'The ninety-five per cent who won't rest until they have one.'

His eyes lit up. 'Aha. But then you'll be forced to have the husband.'

'No, I don't think so.' A grin escaped her when she saw

his bemused expression. 'Not necessarily. It's amazing what women can achieve these days.'

'*Per carita.*'

He looked so thoroughly scandalised she gave way to irrepressible laughter.

'Do you think you might be a tiny bit strait-laced, Valentino?'

'In the case of children, I am in the straitjacket,' he said firmly, his eyes twinkling. 'But in the case of women…' he smiled '…I can be a little more accommodating.'

'That's magnanimous indeed. I know what Lauren would say about that.'

'Lauren.' Valentino turned on her. His eyes hardened, narrowing on her face. 'How did she come to be involved with those people, do you know?'

She stared at him in surprise, jolted by his tone. 'You mean…? Well, I wouldn't say she was involved with them, exactly. They're just friends. Lola has a gallery, I believe, and Lauren's an artist, of course. I'm not sure, but I think it might have been through Giancarlo that she got her television contract. Lola does a lot of entertaining, and—'

His lip curled in a sardonic grimace and she broke off.

'Why? What's wrong with them?'

'Just how much do you trust your cousin?'

'*Valentino.*' She stared at him in disbelief. 'What sort of a question's that? What are you saying?' She grew conscious of people in the street turning their heads to look at them.

He stood quite still and the lines of his face grew stern. His dark eyes were grim and impenetrable, and though he spoke very softly his accent was strongly pronounced. 'I am informing you of this for your own well-being, Pia. Those people are not friends. Not for your cousin, and not for you.'

Stunned, she repeated, 'Why? What's wrong with them?'

His eyes snapped. 'Can you not accept my word for it? You should avoid them.'

To her absolute shock he turned abruptly and strode away,

clambering up the steps with all the lithe agility of a Positanoan born and bred.

She stood paralysed for seconds, watching him out of sight, her heart thumping. What had just happened?

She walked back to the apartment slowly, trying to unravel what had gone wrong, a raw spot in her chest.

Everything had changed. Earlier, with the half-promise of passion in the afternoon, she'd been feeling so buoyant and excited. On the edge of a delicious turning point. A new romance, a new lover. The start of a vibrant new chapter in her life. She'd adored being with him in the café, tingling to the vibrations between them. Being introduced to his acquaintances like a friend.

Then mention Lauren and her friends and it all exploded in her face.

Maybe she was beginning to see a pattern here. Take last night. One minute he was mad for her, hot with desire, the next racing in the opposite direction.

What was wrong with the guy? She just didn't *get* Valentino Silvestri.

Back at the apartment, she took out her notebook and examined her hasty scrawl, her mind whirring with the conversation.

What were his suspicions about? As far as Lauren was concerned she'd stake her cousin against anyone for integrity, courage, professionalism... And as for the Fiorellos. He'd made them sound quite sinister. She couldn't imagine Lauren having anything to do with people who were seedy. Was there was some ancient vendetta between the Silvestris and the Fiorellos?

She opened her sketchbook to a blank page and started to transfer the image with a soft pencil. Strong here, shade there, not forgetting those subtle lines that crinkled in the corners of his eyes when he smiled.

Wishing she had a good clear photo she could work from

to boost her memory, she continued to draw through the afternoon. The manner in which the impulse had stolen over her felt quite like old times. It was so uplifting to know she still had her powers. At last she could feel quietly certain the bountiful well of creativity she'd drawn on all her life was again brimful and revitalised.

Her confidence soared, as if once again the earth had solidified under her feet.

Regardless of Valentino, Euan or any other man who happened to come or go in her life, she had *this*. Nothing could take it from her. Not permanently, she knew that now. Her gift was part of her, warp and weft. No one could cheat her of it, not even a guy in a ski mask.

She was distracted by the sound of the doorbell. Her pulse escalating, she lay down her pencil and closed the sketchbook, slipping it into its protective sleeve.

What now? Another apology? At least she hoped he'd have an explanation for storming off. She'd demand one, at the very least.

In spite of her resolute attitude, her heart quaked a little as she smoothed down her skirt and strolled to the door. Her hand actually shook as she reached for the knob. After the astounding end to what had been shaping up to be a very sexy little encounter she needed to be cool, tone down her reception, and not give the impression of eagerness.

'Yes?' she enquired coldly, only to be taken aback to see a woman outside on the balcony. She was dark-haired and attractive, perhaps in her early to mid thirties. She wore heels and a slim blue dress with wrap-around skirt that fastened at the hip and gave her leanness a sinuous sort of sexiness.

Her full red lips curved in a smile 'You are Pia?'

'Yes.'

She extended her hand. 'I'm Lola Fiorello, Lauren's friend. I promised her I would drop by to welcome her little cousin.' She beamed with such friendliness Pia disguised her wariness and greeted the woman as if she had no suspicion she was welcoming the Wicked Witch of the South.

'*Lola*, of course. Hello. It's great to meet you.' Pia took her hand, but Lola went one better, hugging Pia and kissing her on both cheeks in the European style. Then she opened her capacious bag and produced a bottle of red wine and a fragrant package of coffee beans.

Pleasantly flustered, Pia accepted the gifts with thanks and invited her in. She offered to open the wine, but Lola declined.

'I always drink tea when I visit here,' she explained.

While Pia put the kettle on Lola swished about examining the books and pictures, bombarding Pia with questions about her trip and her impressions of the village.

'Have you met anyone yet? Apart from tourists, of course.'

'A couple of people,' Pia said. 'One of the neighbours and... Tony in the café up in the *piazza*. And a sweet old gentleman named Luigi.'

'Ah, that would be Luigi Salvatore. *Sì, sì, sì, sì, sì.*' She nodded in smiling confirmation. 'He's a nice old guy. Was he all dressed up in his church clothes?'

'He was,' Pia exclaimed. 'How did you know?'

'He needs to go to Mass every morning, so he wears them every day.'

Pia laughed. 'Well, he looked beautiful, anyway. Do you know everyone in the village? You must visit quite a lot.'

Lola smiled. 'I know all the locals because I grew up here.'

'And you're in the film industry?'

'No, that's Giancarlo. I'm an entrepreneur. I collect works of art. Pictures, sculpture for my little gallery at Anacapri. You must come over and see. This is how I've come to know Lauren. Lauren tells me you're a very talented artist yourself. You've had some commissions?'

'Well, yes, a few.'

Pia set the tea things on the coffee table. She wasn't especially keen to talk about her work, not while it was still in convalescence, so to speak.

'I'm so glad you've called,' she said, in a bid to change the subject. 'There are so many things I need to ask someone.' Like how the average macho Italian male thought.

Lola sat on the sofa. 'Black, please. Fantastic. Oh, I love these. That lemon filling is so…so…' She took a tiny bite of the puff, and her blissful expression said the rest. 'Now,' she said, after swallowing and dabbing at her mouth with a napkin. 'I want to invite you to lunch on the twenty-fourth. I will send Dominico to meet you at the pier at twelve. Here…' She turned and plunged into her bag, bringing out a small notebook. She scribbled something. 'Look for the *Sirocco*. And here's the number you call in case we get lost. There.' She tore off the page and handed it to Pia. 'Oh, and bring your toothbrush. It will be a party, just a few little people from the industry, a little relaxation, some entertainment, and we need plenty of beautiful girls.' She beamed.

Pia blinked. 'That's very kind of you…'

She was wearing a smile, but her risk sensors were madly signalling. A party at the home of a wealthy movie director on Capri was, of course, exciting. No doubt the most intriguing party invitation she'd ever received. But…

Lunch was one thing, but a whole weekend? Stuck on an island with *strangers*?

Her inner coward burst to the fore. Sure, she was supposed to avoid avoidance, but, despite Lola's charm and the fact that it sounded like *fun*, was Pia Renfern really ready for fun to this degree? A concentrated burst of heavy socialising?

She racked her brains for a credible excuse. Lola wasn't the sort of woman who took no for an answer. The forceful woman was still chattering on, painting a vivid picture of the glittering revelry in store, when the doorbell rang again.

Pia started and every one of her nerves galvanised. This time it could only be Valentino. She dropped her lemon cream puff and rose, parties on Capri pushed from the forefront of her mind.

What would he say? Would he apologise? What would *she* say?

She braced herself, her hands trembling, then opened the door, breathless. Valentino was leaning back against the balustrade, his thumb tucked into the pocket of his jeans, looking serious, and so darkly handsome her insides plunged at once into a dark yearning turmoil. But it was pure lust, she reminded herself. Not murk.

He appraised her with a deep searing glance. 'I'm not disturbing you?'

As *if* her heart acted like that every day. 'Not at all.'

'Do you have some time to talk?'

'Yes. Sure. Of course.' Her brain coughed into life. For a moment she almost felt guilty when she remembered Lola, but for heaven's sake. Did she have to apologise for her cousin's choice of friends? 'Though as a matter of fact, I have a visitor. It's Lola,' she added steadily.

His face darkened and she said hurriedly, 'But you're welcome to come in and join us. Please. By all means.' She opened the door wide.

His eyes narrowed, then he straightened and followed her inside, pausing at the entrance to the sitting room.

Pia attempted a gracious introduction. 'Lola, do you know— Valentino? Er, Valentino...'

Lola looked up from her sofa and her dark eyes widened infinitesimally. 'Why, Tino,' she exclaimed after a heartbeat. 'This is a surprise. So you have come home at last. You are on vacation?' She smiled, while her sharp assessing gaze flicked rapidly from Valentino to Pia and back again.

Pia noticed that Valentino's face hardened, though he accepted the winged chair she offered him with his usual cool grace. 'You could call it that,' he said in measured tones. 'And you, Lola? Still doing—what you do?' The edge in his voice drew Pia's glance again, and with a slight shock she saw that despite his politeness his eyes were like black ice.

Lola's considerable lashes descended halfway. '*Sì*, Tino. My little gallery is doing quite well, thank you. And you... Are you still with the navy? Chasing pirates and catching all those naughty smugglers?'

'Not any more. I am with a global company now.' His white teeth flashed, though his smile held no warmth.

There was a slight gap in the flow of conversation, more of a fissure, really, perhaps even a schism, then Lola enquired, 'Your—grandfather is well?'

Valentino said politely, 'As well as can be expected of an old man who has suffered pain and the tragedy of public disgrace and dishonour.'

Lola's face stiffened, then she turned to Pia. 'Are you working on anything at the moment, Pia? Lauren tells me you have had some success with portraits.'

Pia felt acutely aware of Valentino's glance shooting her way.

'Some,' she said, colouring. 'Though I'm not restricted to portraiture. I've tried a bit of everything.' She added lightly, 'And, no, I'm not working at the moment.'

Lola arched her brows and smiled cajolingly. 'Ah, but I think you must while you are here. Wait until you come over to Capri. You'll be inspired. It's a perfect spot for painters. Don't you agree, Tino?'

Valentino held Lola's eyes. 'I don't recommend it.'

A dull flush stained Lola's cheeks and she broke into a stream of impassioned Italian to which Valentino replied in kind in a cold, punishing tone. They spoke so quickly Pia couldn't catch any meaning, though at one point Valentino said 'ariana' and the word appeared to anger Lola deeply, because she broke off, collected her bag and scarf, and abruptly rose to her feet.

Dismayed by the strange conversation and Valentino's

astounding rudeness to someone who was, after all, her guest, Pia said, 'What do you mean, Valentino? Why don't you recommend it?'

'Yes, Tino.' Lola reverted to English, mockery in her smile. 'Why not? Many *artisti* visit our villa. Artists have been inspired by Capri for thousands of years. Why shouldn't Pia?'

There was a challenge in her smile that Valentino ignored. Instead he turned to Pia. 'You wouldn't like it there.'

'Why not?'

He hesitated a second, then he said coolly, 'Because you are afraid of high places. You will admit, Lola, your villa is precariously placed on that cliff edge.'

Lola turned to Pia with a little cry. 'Oh, is this true, darling?'

The air felt punched from Pia's lungs. She knew she'd turned scarlet. 'No, n-no—*Well*, I...' Her shiny, new, cool, confident self was blasted into fragments. She had a shaming vision of the whole painful gamut of her disorder getting out and being broadcast around the town, people *knowing*. Luckily, somehow pride rushed to her defences.

She fired Valentino a glowering glance. 'I can't imagine where you got that idea from, Valentino. You could say *this* villa is precariously placed. This entire town.' She turned to Lola. 'I will come to the party. Thank you, Lola, I'd love to.'

Valentino turned to her, his black brows bristling, but she ignored him.

'That's wonderful, darling,' Lola said, flashing Valentino a sly triumphant glance. 'I will so look forward to it.' An amused smile played on her lips. 'Valentino can stay over here and worry about you over there in the big bad villa.' She gave a silvery laugh and moved to the door, trailing a farewell with a backwards waggle of her long nails. '*Ciao*. Don't forget your pyjamas. If you wear them, of course,' she added with another laugh.

She cast a mischievous glance back at Valentino. 'Our

parties are famous, aren't they, Tino? On second thoughts, why don't you come too? Catch up with some old friends. You know you are always welcome at the Villa Fiorello.' She winked.

Valentino appeared not to notice Lola's parting gibes, instead continuing to look at Pia.

Pia evaded his curious gaze. Still numb with shock, she walked outside with her guest to the balcony and down the steps to the courtyard. Betrayal, that was what it had amounted to. What sort of man brought up a person's private anxiety and shouted it to the world? Was he just another Euan, so set on his own agenda he failed to take into account that other people had feelings?

All the way to the gate Lola chattered blithely about a dozen inconsequential things Pia failed to take in, then she stopped and placed her hand on Pia's arm.

'Be very careful of him, darling,' Lola said softly. 'He is a dangerous man. He can hurt you.'

A pang cut through Pia. 'In what way?'

'In the usual way of men. If he wants something, if he goes after something, he is relentless. But he will never love you.'

CHAPTER EIGHT

Pia walked upstairs, fury gathering in her like a swarm of bees. She faced Valentino, shaking, barely able to see him through the red-hot mist of her anger.

'How could you?' Her low voice trembled with the depth of her emotion. 'Why did you have to tell Lola that? Do you have any sensitivity at all?'

His brows elevated and he threw up his hands. 'Sensitivity? *Sì*, I have sensitivity. I'm very sensitive to the *truth*.'

His lack of remorse only fuelled her wrath. 'Why did you even have to bring it up? Just because I—I was tired after the flight when you were speeding along those narrow roads…'

He stiffened. 'I was not speeding. I *never* speed. I'm a responsible guy and I uphold the law at all times. I was driving you safely, and I think if you are honest you will admit that in the times when you weren't flirting with me you were as nervous as a kitten.'

'*Flirting…?*' She spluttered the demeaning word. 'That's your imagination. As if I would flirt with a—a total *stranger*.'

He took a step closer to her, his dark eyes glittering, forcing her to step back towards the wall. 'Was it my imagination that as soon as you were out of the car you were kissing me as if there was no tomorrow until you had an attack of free-spirited conscience? And was it my imagination last night when you were too afraid to walk into your own apartment? Did I imagine that five minutes later you were melting in my arms like mozzarella? You'd have offered more than mere kisses to keep me here with you.'

The wicked words only further lacerated her wounded sensibilities.

'All right, mock if you like,' she said, her throat thickening, shamed that even in this extremity she was almost unbearably aware of his long powerful thighs a handspan from her own. Another move and his hard body could have crushed her to the wall. Despite her angry pride, deep inside her, from some primitive recess, a hot vibration sizzled through her erotic zones like a shooting star. 'I might have been a bit nervous. I thought you might understand that some people have feelings about such things. I was mistaken, obviously.' Emotion made her voice unreasonably husky. 'I'd started to think you might be different. Someone I could trust. I thought you were—nice.'

An electric stillness came over him, like a leopard distracted from the carcass it was savaging by a more fascinating prey. Her heart started to thump. She became preternaturally aware of the five o'clock shadow on his lean jaw, the sensuousness of his sexy mouth. He was so close she could feel the heat from his big lean body.

If he touched her, she was afraid she might combust.

His voice deepened, and she noticed his accent seemed more pronounced. 'And I thought *you* were nice,' he said, his dark eyes shimmering with an intense and mesmerising light. 'I still think you are—nice.'

On his tongue the word acquired an almost sexual inflection.

The air tautened, and she felt a warning tingle in her breasts and other intimate parts. His lean hands closed around her arms like circlets of fire. She could have shaken him off, but his touch seemed necessary to her enchanted flesh.

He dragged her up against him and brought his mouth down on hers in a passionate possession that sucked all the breath from her body. Her pride lost its wish to fight the sexy onslaught and succumbed.

The taste of his lips, his breath mingling with hers, his iron-hard frame in friction with her softness, and in an instant she was drunk with him and his devastating masculinity.

She didn't just surrender. With a deep growl in her throat she ravished him in return with her lips and hands, with her hungry writhing body, fastening him to her with all at her disposal.

He broke the kiss, barely in the nick of time to save her from suffocation.

'Now what?' she gasped, her voice deep, almost guttural, after dragging in a couple of breaths. 'Is this where you—?' She was going to say 'Walk out?' but he didn't wait for her to finish.

He swept her up into his arms and carried her forcibly into the bedroom. Too shocked at first to react, Pia found the contact with his vibrant sexy body was over too soon. By the time she'd found some actual words he was holding her suspended over her bed.

'Just what do you think you're *doing*?' Her voice was practically a moan, because deep inside her a tremor of the utmost wanton yearning was inflaming her flesh.

He dropped her in the middle of the bed and started stripping off his shirt, his jeans, his underpants. She drank in the honed beauty of his wide powerful chest, his washboard abs and lean hips, her avid eyes widening further at every stage until she saw the majestic extent of his erection, its engorged thickness and commanding length. With a total lack of pretension he produced a foil packet from his jeans, tore it open with his teeth, and sat on the bed to sheathe himself.

Her lips dried.

Prepared for action, he flung himself on the bed and held her down. '*This* is what I am doing.' Desire blazed in his dark eyes like fire. 'I am testing to see if this bed is as bouncy and springy as the claims that have been made about it.'

With smouldering purpose, he yanked the end of the laces securing her blouse and pulled the bodice apart. She had to assist him a little to unfasten her bra, but when it was all off and her breasts were free his enthusiasm was flattering, and thrilling.

His voice was a groan. *'La vostra bellezza...'*

'What? What does that *mean*?' she breathed.

'Can't you guess? It means you are beautiful, you have beautiful breasts... They are so ripe, so sweet... *Mio Dio*, you make me so *hot*.'

He kissed them, then with an expeditiousness she could only give him credit for, he pushed up her skirt and nipped her undies down to her ankles. Then he paused, his eyes ablaze, while she lay panting and exposed, her entire body in a fever, on the brink, the delicious yearning brink, and hopefully...

His eyes glowed. 'Now we will see how I can make you happy.'

A tiny shade of doubt assailed her. Could he...? Could *she*...? With her history, shouldn't she warn him, at least?

Softly he stroked her most delicate tissues, sending piquant little frissons of rapturous excitement through every vital nerve ending. She was so hot for him his every light touch incited a frenzy of fire in her burning flesh.

So far, so good. But she still had a conscience. What if her passion deserted her at the last critical moment?

She drew a deep breath. 'There's just one thing...'

He scanned her face, his dark eyes tender. 'You worry too much.'

Then with supreme untrammelled confidence he positioned his lean powerful body over her, supporting himself on his arms, and with one smooth slick thrust buried himself inside her.

She thrilled when she heard his groan of pleasure. The *relief.*

Then he paused a moment to allow her to accustom herself, gazing down at her with amused enquiry.

'Are we okay?'

A quick examination of her symptoms told her only that she felt fine and voluptuously suspended. In fact, she felt filled to a languorous perfection, and smiled.

He made a seductive little move. A tingling sweetness shot through her. Ah-h-h, delicious, but she craved more, *more*, *MORE*. He started to rock her, gently at first, then firmer, and faster, and with every magic stroke she felt a searing pleasure sizzle through her like a ray of violent light.

'How nice am I now?' he said.

'Oh-h-h, you're nice.'

'You feel so good,' he said thickly. 'I've never been so hot for a woman.'

His encouraging words incited multiple rays of the divine and searing pleasure, and she participated in the sexy rhythm, wrapping her legs around him in passionate cooperation.

He plunged and plunged, stroking her inner walls, and her orgasm began to swell inside her, slowly at first, then like a storm, a wild and furious tempest in her senses, until at last she reached her glorious climax and shattered in an explosion of rapture.

A heartbeat later Valentino shuddered into his climax in her arms with gratifying conviction.

Afterwards they lay together in the soft twilight, her pale arms and legs entangled with his bronzed hairy limbs. He was more beautiful even than she'd dreamed, for this moment his chiselled profile, the planes and angles of his muscled body hers to trace and touch.

Sometimes he kissed her shoulder, her breast. Wrapped in a golden bliss of happiness and the most profound relief, she savoured every precious nuance. Thank the Lord and the entire heavenly line-up her hex had been broken. There'd been no failure and she'd done no harm. She suffered no recriminations, only tenderness, affection, and a deep vibrant connection almost frightening in its pull.

Valentino kept looking, needing to feast his eyes on her supple beauty. Her soft mouth, rosy with kissing, the sweet round swells of her breasts, the heavenly triangle of her pelvis and pale slender limbs. If he had any discomfort it was in his soul, or whatever part his conscience inhabited.

He shouldn't have, but, *perdio*, he was only human, wasn't he?

Still, he needed to evaluate his position.

A woman with intolerable associations had come across his path and he'd succumbed. But only once. If Lola hadn't appeared today, in the deceitful, treacherous flesh, he could have relied on his instincts and enjoyed Pia Renfern to the zenith of sensual delight. If only Pia had shown no interest in pursuing the poisonous association. He'd warned her, hadn't he? He'd done his best.

As it was...

'What is it? Why are you looking so grim?' She raised herself on one elbow to look down at him, and trailed her fingers through his chest hair. 'Aren't I giving you enough attention?' Smiling, she bent to kiss his nipple, enticement in her blue eyes, her ripe lips.

A tremor shivered through him and he felt his eager flesh make a fateful stir. Her lips trailed lower, down his abdomen towards his navel, where she paused and looked up at him, her eyes brimful of laughter and promise, and something else. Something he must not allow to exist there. 'Aren't you glad you stayed?'

He felt his chest twinge at the same time as the stir threatened to become a full-on revival. Temptation warred with his conscience. *Sacramento*, what was he, an honourable man who used a woman he must withdraw from?

There was still time to minimise the damage.

With a superhuman effort of will, he raised himself and reached to touch her face. 'Pia, *tesoro*…'

She stared at him, startlement in her eyes, then he drew away from her, slung his legs over the side of the bed and reached for his clothes.

'Oh.' The shock in her voice made him flinch. 'You're leaving?'

He paused, half angled away from her, and avoided her eyes. 'I would love to stay with you, *tesoro*, truly, I am broken-hearted to leave, but there is something I must do this evening.'

The moment of charged silence told him how it must look to her. A quick hook-up before dinner, cold, casual and mechanical. He noticed her reach for the sheet and wrap it around her nakedness as though shamed.

Quickly he put on his underwear, his jeans, his discomfort painful.

She lifted her shoulders and said with careful casualness, 'There's no need to be broken-hearted. It was only sex, after all.'

Guilt stabbed him and he paused in the act of pulling on his shirt to gaze at her. Her eyes met his, unreadable, swirling with feminine mystery. 'Pia, you don't think in those terms. I don't believe even you feel like that.'

She was holding the sheet tightly to her breasts as if to wipe out his having seen and enjoyed them. She lifted her chin a little. 'Even me? How do you know what I think, Valentino? *Feel*.' She made light of it, rolled her eyes, but he could hear the knowledge in her voice of how the joyous moment had been doused.

He met her eyes. The truth had to be laid on the line before things went too far. 'I have to be honest. I'm not in a position to offer a woman anything. I travel for my work and…I'm in town a few days only.'

Her sparkling smile ripped through him. 'Well, then, I guess I'll put my order for the wedding invitations on hold.' Despite her proud sarcasm, the huskiness in her voice grabbed him in a place he'd prefer not to have had his attention drawn to at that precise moment. She continued to pile on the pain, musing, 'And there was I, thinking I'd trapped a live one.'

He felt as if his bare ass were being hauled very gently across burning coals.

He racked his brains for a graceful exit. 'Please don't think… You are not just any woman. You are—so beautiful… Charming, intelligent…'

She flushed and he knew how clumsy his words were. What a despicable *carogna*.

'Please don't worry, Valentino. I'm fine. I came here as a tourist, didn't I? Not to lose my heart to any of the natives. I'd never make that silly mistake. Go on your merry way, my man, and be happy. This is how we free spirits prefer it.'

Despite her grin and her humorous tone the twinge pinched him again. For an instant he felt an almost unbearable urge to take her in his arms, but once he did that…

'Go, please. *Hurry.*' She waved him away, and he understood she was serious in her need to have him out of her sight. 'You don't want to be late.'

He hesitated, then leaned across and kissed her averted cheek. 'I'll see you.'

Then like the conflicted criminal he was, he escaped.

CHAPTER NINE

PIA brooded.

How ungrateful was she anyway, to care that a man she felt madly attracted to could take her or leave her? Take her *and* leave her, that was. She hadn't even been sure until that fantastic hour in his arms whether or not she was completely back to normal.

Now she knew she *was*, she should be looking on the bright side. *Should* be. Instead, she was yearning. Yearning, regretting and reliving the moments. Going over in her mind every single thing he'd said to her. Speculating about the hostility that existed between him and Lola. Something had happened there. As for Lola's warning...

When had a warning ever worked?

And who ever made such a warning anyway, except a woman with an agenda? She wished she'd had an opportunity to ask him to explain his extraordinary behaviour towards Lola. The only thing she could think of—well, it stood to reason, didn't it?—was that they had once been lovers and had had a bitter parting.

But Lola was married now. Surely old loves didn't remain explosive for years. Take her own case. She might have become disillusioned with Euan and been in pain for some time after he walked out, but anger required too much energy to maintain for very long.

Sure, Valentino seemed too hostile to the woman for

comfort, but from Pia's point of view Lola should stop fluttering her lashes at him. In fact, it struck her that if she hadn't been a peace-loving animal she'd have quite liked to remove Lola's lashes. One by one and with physical force, if necessary.

She spent a day or two on her balcony creating a wistful little watercolour when it was obvious Positano demanded the bold sensuousness of oils, then realised she was sliding back into her old habit of avoidance. Trying to avoid life in all its miserable glory.

Avoiding Valentino.

The sad thing was it was hurting more *not* to see him than it would have been to see him and not be able to have him. At least, she thought so.

But… Her glass was half full. He had at least fancied her for a few moments, even if he didn't consider her a keeper. She might not be someone he'd choose to take to a desert island with him, but she was at least good enough for a quick toss before dinner. How many women could claim that?

She pushed that disquieting door firmly shut.

She made a strong and definite resolution to get over Valentino Silvestri and embrace life fully, starting the very next day.

Looking on the bright side, taken all in all, murk notwithstanding, she wasn't doing so badly in the recovery stakes.

Desire was back with a vengeance, painting on its way. There were other menaces she could stare down as well to fully seal her confidence. Sailing would be conquered when she went to Capri, though she didn't care to think too much about what other challenges lay in wait for her there. Cliffs were fairly well catered for on her daily walks.

How about swimming?

She was no world-class athlete, but the weather was warm and she'd always loved a plunge in the surf. She wouldn't dream of risking making a fool of herself on the main beach where the tourists flocked, but she'd noticed a tiny little section of beach down at the bottom of the steps carved into the hillside between the villas. She could test herself there, just wade in up to her knees at first, maybe even her waist—anyway, as far as she could go without scaring herself to death.

Luckily, in a burst of pre-flight optimism she'd thought to pack her one-piece with the cut-out sides. She dragged it out and draped it over a chair in hopeful readiness.

Her resolve weakened a bit overnight, but after some vacillating she steeled herself to get up early before anyone was about. Shivering a little in the cool dawn air, she pulled on the swimsuit, then slathered on some sunscreen, donned shorts and a top and grabbed one of Lauren's towels.

It was still too early for most tourists except a few dedicated exercise freaks, and there was no sign of life at the Silvestri stronghold. Before she lost her nerve she whisked downstairs and across the courtyard to the side gate.

The steps down to the shore between the houses were steep, with bits of wild creeper sticking up here and there to trip the unwary and dips in the middle worn smooth from centuries of feet.

She crept past the black wrought iron gate to Valentino's villa, hardly daring to breathe. Rounding the last curve and arriving at the bottom step, she stepped onto the tiny pebbled beach—in fact it was barely a beach, merely a break in the formidable base of the cliff—and her insides jolted into disarray.

The space was occupied. Powerfully occupied, in fact. Valentino was on the pebbly sand, his arms resting on his bent knees, gazing out to sea to where the big yacht was riding at anchor.

He glanced around, immobilising for one electric instant when he saw it was her. It was only an instant, but it jarred through her like a javelin.

Her first impulse was to retreat back up the steps. Did she want him to think she was pursuing him like some pathetic groupie? But he pushed his sunglasses back onto his head as if intending to speak. Sheer good manners held her there for just that instant, and her window of opportunity to escape closed.

As she advanced a pace the images of their shared passion seemed to dominate the space and suck out all the air. She had an overwhelming sense that he was thinking of it too. Her nudity. His.

He was unshaven, and she couldn't help noticing how his beard outlined the chiselled lines of his mouth. Sensuous.

She moistened her lips. 'Hi.'

'Buongiorno.' Their voices collided.

He got up and bent casually to pick up his towel, reminding her of his athletic suppleness. She tried not to let her glance drift below the level of his chin, but she was glad the tee shirt was longish. She didn't want to be reminded of pleasures past, never to be recaptured. There was no avoiding his gorgeous manly chest though, partly visible through wet patches in the shirt. The whorls of black hair she'd twisted around her fingers.

The same black hair that had grazed her naked breasts.

He didn't grant her a similar courtesy of avoidance. His eyes flicked over her with frank sexual appreciation, as if her curves and feminine assets were her most significant attributes. *Men.*

She reached for the first words she could find. 'I didn't expect to see you here. I thought you said you were only staying a few days.'

He shrugged. 'How many is a few?' After a second he added rather stiffly, 'I didn't notice you around yesterday. I wondered if you had gone somewhere.'

'No.' She looked down. 'I—was working.'

'Painting?'

She nodded and pushed some pebbles around with the toe of her sandal.

He studied her face, then moved a step nearer. 'I noticed you drawing in the café. It must be wonderful to be an artist.

To have such an ability.' His beautiful hands imbued his every statement with sincerity.

'Sometimes it's wonderful,' she acknowledged, angling her gaze towards the cliff. 'Most of the time it's—not.'

Like life, she could have added. Or falling in love.

'You didn't say anything about being an artist when we were driving here.' He looked keenly at her, and she lifted her shoulders carelessly.

She wished his every nuance didn't ache inside her, like his Italian vowels and the way his accent turned artist into 'artista'. Or the way his long lashes screened his gaze when he didn't want her to guess what he was thinking. As if she'd ever had a hope in hell of that.

Perhaps she wasn't seeming very friendly, perhaps even rather cold, but it was awkward knowing one was only a temporary fixture. An *amuse bouche* rather than a main, so to speak.

He persevered, a smile on his sexy mouth. 'Do you paint on your balcony? I thought I saw your blonde hair there the other morning, shining in the sun like Giulietta.'

She lifted a brow. 'Julietta who?'

He gestured. 'Giulietta—in Shakespeare.'

'Oh, her.' She made a tight grimace. 'I hope not. She died young, you know.'

'Ah,' he said with an apologetic spreading of his hands. 'She wasn't a good example. Perhaps if your hair had been longer I could call you Rapunzel.'

She gave him a long withering look. 'Lucky for me I prefer my hair short.'

A silence fell. He gazed out at the sea, and she sensed he was feeling the strain. All at once she felt sorry for him. What a mad, cruel, cold, psychotic bitch she was being. Her heart was actually paining in sympathy for the discomfort womanly pride and honour was forcing her to inflict, when he said, 'Are you intending to swim now?'

He glanced back at her, his sensual gaze flicking all over her with maximum penetration. X-raying through her clothes to her swimsuit, no doubt. And through that to her bare flesh. Flesh he had enjoyed.

'To swim? Well, yes, I mean, not necessarily to *swim*. I suppose I'm…intending—'

He frowned, interrupting. '*Sì?* But would you say you are a competent swimmer, Pia?'

She felt a jolt of surprise. What?

She stared at him while he took the opportunity to make another flickering assessment, ostensibly measuring her muscle tone, floatability and the depth of her lungs, though more likely reacquainting himself with her breasts, hips and other parts deemed good enough for an hour's entertainment.

Another suspicion struck her then, that with her pale, washed-out appearance she might not look all that athletic. Possibly she didn't, but her pride was piqued. Hadn't she once won the Under Sixteens' silver for treading water at the Year Eleven swimming carnival?

'Certainly,' she said, injecting some hauteur into her voice. 'Though I'm not sure why you ask, Valentino.'

'Just so you know, the sea here has some very strong currents.'

It hadn't escaped her notice that his hair was wet and droplets of water still glistened on his bronzed thighs, as if it wasn't long since he'd been braving the currents himself. A surge of anger shot through her. The nerve. Obviously she was no daredevil, a publicly certified chicken in fact, but was he trying to rub her face in it?

'Thank you for your concern,' she said on a down-sweep of her lashes, adding with a cold laugh, 'Though no doubt the sea has some very strong currents everywhere.'

His lips pressed together, then he shrugged and made a gesture towards the sea as if it were within his personal gift. 'By all means, then, if you have no fear.'

'I have no fear,' she retorted with an angry smile, heat flushing her cheeks.

He threw up his hands in a gesture that said very clearly he'd tried his best but who could reason with a woman like her? Then he spread his towel and sat down again.

She stared, taken aback. She'd assumed he was leaving. Was he planning now to stay and watch her?

Quickly she scanned the water—the enormous water. Whoever said the sheltered waters of the Bay of Naples were placid? It was the Tyrrhenian Sea, for goodness' sake, and turbulent. There were waves boiling into the little cove, hissing out again, and she suspected that along there at the cliff's edges where the waves were smashing themselves the water was deep. Seriously deep.

If he stayed there she would be forced to go in. Not only to wade in a little way, as she'd planned, but to swim.

She moved a way along the beach, creating a few metres of definite distance between them, hoping he'd take the hint, then wasted a bit of time pretending to survey the pebbles and the huge rocks at the base of the nearby cliff. Little frills of foam lapped the edge of the sand, and she supposed she could inch her way into it for a couple of metres. Clearly he'd been about to leave before. Maybe by the time she got up to her knees he'd be gone.

Though maybe she should just ignore him and go home. Who cared what he thought, anyway? She felt such a longing to turn tail and run for cover, but his public announcement about her cowardice was still raw. She steeled herself.

The worst part was having to undress. She might have been wearing her one-piece, but the air was rife with vibrations. Though he was staying put at his end of the beach, she could feel his glance scorching her through his sunglasses.

Glass magnified heat ten times, she'd once read, and she believed it. By the time she got home she'd have third-degree burns.

It was better to be quick and have the ordeal over, so, bracing for it, she whipped off her top, then unzipped her shorts and let them fall. As she stepped out of them she'd hardly ever felt more exposed. Why hadn't she smoothed on some fake tan? Nothing looked more naked than white skin.

She could feel his gaze searing down her spine like a blowtorch.

She cast a surreptitious look back to see if he was watching and he *was*. In fact he'd taken his glasses off to get the clearest possible view. She met his bold, sexy gaze, smouldering hot and amused, as if he *knew* and was enjoying how self-conscious he was making her feel. How—sensual.

A bolt of red-hot anger roiled through her. How dared he?

Fine, *signore*, she hissed mentally, gritting her teeth as steam issued from her ears. She straightened to stand tall, shoulders back, tummy in, stretched her arms up to give him a chance to check out her curves, and adjusted the edges of her swimsuit at her breasts and bottom in case he'd forgotten her best bits. She drew her fingers through her hair and ruffled it. See all you can, Valentino Silvestri. Enjoy.

She left her clothes in a neat pile on the towel, then walked firmly down to the edge. The sand was grey blue and charcoal, more like fragmented pumice, in fact, and not so soothing on tender feet. It was the least of her worries.

The first shock of the waves chilled her toes, but she kept on. She was boiling with such rage the water around her might have sizzled, but she hardly noticed, only aware that the further in she went, the less Valentino could see of her. The pebbly bottom had a steep slope, and with surprisingly few steps the water level rose to her knees, then her hips. She was in nearly as far as her waist and still furious when she stepped off the pebbly shelf and into the deep, deep sea.

The deep swallowed her cry as it closed over her head. She kicked and struggled for minutes, *how* she struggled to gain the surface again and breathe. For dreadful suffocating moments she flailed wildly, suspended in the churning underwater.

She did at last burst through into the light before her lungs exploded. She gasped in a breath and went under again, but, having made the surface once, some automatic part of her brain remembered the water-treading motion and set her body to action, treading and puffing.

Were there sharks in the Tyrrhenian Sea? She should have found that out, but she was grateful not to be drowning, at least. Keeping her head just above water, she noticed that she'd drifted a surprising way out from the little inlet in that short time. Valentino was still there, watching her, sitting forward now, alert.

It was all his fault.

'Go away,' she yelled with all her might. 'Go *aw*—' A wave swamped her then and filled her mouth, nose, head, and the entire universe with salt water.

When her choking gasps had subsided, she noticed Valentino on his feet, staring intently at her. She started to breast-stroke to demonstrate she *could* swim to shore, but couldn't seem to make much headway. She gave up being graceful then and swam as strongly as she could with more vicious little waves slapping her in the face, but almost imperceptibly, relentlessly, she felt herself being tugged towards the jagged cliffs at the end of the beach.

The familiar panic gripped her lungs. In an attempt to power out of the situation, she tried to take charge of it by changing to freestyle, changing direction, but it was hard to breathe while panicking, and she'd swallowed a bit of water at some point and didn't quite have the strength to fight the current.

Yes, she could freely admit now to any man who wanted to mock her, there *was* a current. A powerful current racing her towards those cliffs.

Despite her thrashing efforts, before she knew it they loomed frighteningly near, towering above her with awful menace.

Something scraped her knee and she let out a shriek, then she felt something grab her at her waist. Startled out of her terrified skin, she twisted around to see what had her in its jaws. Through a curtain of water she glimpsed the face of a man.

He pulled her close, holding her against his chest. Horror at being forced in such proximity to his big strong body set off some crazy reflex in her brain, and she struggled against him, then with all her might punched him.

He grabbed her flailing fist. *'Calmi,'* he roared. 'I am rescuing you. Here, turn this way and kick your legs.'

He changed his grip then, swiftly switching her into the classic lifesaving position, where she was helpless to struggle as he towed her into the shore.

He helped her up onto the pebbles and patted her back while she sagged onto her knees and coughed up her guts. Well, half of the Bay of Napoli, at least. She was almost surprised not to see crabs and little starfish dislodge from her lungs. When the coughing paroxysm had eased, she managed a watery, 'It's all right. I'm fine.'

Valentino Silvestri smoothed her hair and dabbed her face with her towel, then wrapped it around her shoulders and murmured soothing things in English and Italian. 'Rest here, rest a while.' He knelt beside her and continued to pat her and rub her back. His warm strong hand was comforting, she may as well admit. She might well have started to purr if he'd continued in that soothing vein, but after a few minutes he said, 'Are you all right, Pia? Can you stand?'

'Of course,' she said, feeling as energised as a jellyfish. 'I'm fine. Absolutely fine.'

She made a shaky effort to stand. Truth to tell, her legs were wobbly and she might have weaved a bit. 'There's nothing wrong with me,' she gasped as he propped her up with his strong hands, his dark eyes brimming with concern. God, it was mortifying.

Teeth chattering, she locked the towel around her breasts.

'You didn't have to rescue me. I would have been all right once I—found my—stroke.'

Valentino's eyes glinted, and when she pulled away from him to stoop and gather up her clothes and sandals he watched with a little twist to his mouth. She looked narrowly at him. There was a cut under his eye she hadn't noticed before with something of a bruise, though it was hard to tell with his tan. He must have scraped his face.

'We need to put antiseptic on that leg,' he said firmly.

She blinked to see a nasty graze above her knee, blood trickling down.

'Oh, that? It's nothing.'

But he ignored her weak protest. And of course it did need antiseptic. Toxic bacteria were swarming all over it already and diving into her bloodstream to give her a massive dose of septicaemia, but it was the 'we' she was resisting.

'You just worry about yourself,' she argued, blue and shaking, her chin wobbling uncontrollably. 'Look at you. You've done something to your eye. It's getting all puffy.'

'Is it?' he growled. He compressed his lips with grim severity.

'You look as if someone gave you an almighty whack.'

'Someone did.'

'Who? Oh, you mean...*me*?'

'Forget it,' he said curtly.

She felt dismayed, utterly shamed. Who would have thought Pia Renfern could give a man a black eye? The very idea was so surreal that in her delirium she felt an urgent desire to laugh.

'I'm so sorry.' She tried to hold her smile in, but try as she might the laughter bubbled up and she couldn't prevent a chuckle from escaping. 'Oh, sorry. Honestly. I thought you were a shark.'

'*Cosa?*' Unamused, he stared at her. 'A *shark*?'

'Yes, well, when you grabbed me like that...' Another chuckle burst out, then a couple more, but with a massive effort she reined the rest in when she saw his austere expression. 'Anyway, that's what you do. You—punch them in the face and they—let you go.'

'*Some* of them.' He clipped the words rather savagely.

'Yes. Some.' She cast down her eyes for fear the laugh would explode again. Her cheeks ached with the effort of remaining grave. There was nothing left with which to fill up the grim silence except babble, so she turned to that.

'These pebbles are cruel on your feet. In Australia we have sand, the real thing. Lovely long white beaches of soft, white, really soft...'

'Tell that to Vesuvius,' he interrupted. *'Andiamo.'*

There was a sudden bracing note of command in his voice she might have taken exception to if she'd had more energy. He steered her along for a few steps as she huddled into her towel, picking her quavery way across the pebbles to the steps. She hesitated, shivering and looking up, wondering how she would ever manage the climb.

Clearly Valentino hated waiting. He made an impatient little sound, then swung her up in his arms and carried her up the steps, pausing only to push open the ornate black iron gate with his shoulder and haul her inside.

The only regrettable part of being pressed against his vibrant, strong, manly body was that she was really a little too *non compos mentis* to extract the maximum amount of enjoyment out of it.

CHAPTER TEN

IN ORDINARY circumstances Pia wouldn't have chosen to enter the villa of a man who'd warned her off as if she were a love-struck schoolgirl. Neither would she bathe in his tub, or allow herself to be persuaded into his big leather recliner and swaddled in a blanket. But the circumstances were far from ordinary.

She could have been dashed to pieces on those rocks, so even if Valentino Silvestri was a ruthless misogynist who used women then cast them aside like old socks, she had to give him some credit for jumping in to rescue her. He would hardly have done it with the intention of attempting a repeat performance of their doomed affair. This situation was for first-aid purposes only. Nothing more than that.

She had nothing to reproach herself with.

These were the dim muddled thoughts she soothed herself with anyway, while Valentino ushered her firmly through rooms with walls of pale stone and beautiful old vaulted ceilings to a bathroom.

'You're in shock,' he said while she sagged against the pipes, shivering in her tottery state, staring blankly as the water level rose. 'We need to get you warm. Here, drink this.'

He pressed a glass of some yellowish liquid into her hand.
'What is it?'

'Limoncello. Sip it slowly, now. *Piano, piano.*'

She sipped and something like a sledgehammer slammed

the back of her head. Still, once it was down the liqueur had a lovely lemony flavour. 'Wow,' she gasped, taking another sip.

'*Basta.*' He frowned, whipping the glass away from her before it could reach her lips a third time and placing it on the marble vanity.

Even to a woman in a state of shock the bathroom felt overcrowded. Though it was spacious enough, with its vaulted stone ceiling, large mirrors and a huge old-fashioned tub on croc feet, perhaps because he was still in swimming trunks Valentino took up all the air and the space. Wherever she looked he was there with his long powerful thighs, bronzed, sinewy arms, in the mirrors and in the hard, lean flesh close by her until her senses whirled. Though he took painstaking care not to allow even the tips of the curly black hairs on his limbs to brush her as he showed her where things were kept, his very constraint made the air crackle with tension.

Somehow he managed to avoid looking at her, though her wan reflection was bouncing at him from all directions until the rising steam misted the mirrors.

'I will leave you,' he said abruptly once the bath was ready, with a last glance from beneath his thick black lashes that didn't quite touch her.

Just as well, because she looked a sight. He ejected himself through the door so swiftly it was clear he couldn't wait to escape. When he was gone the room breathed again and became quite spacious, as if a bomb had been defused.

She locked the door after him, though even without the lock she'd have had no hesitation about undressing and easing into the water. Valentino was highly unlikely to come bursting through that door. In her experience, guys found reasons to steer well clear of needy women.

Her graze stung a little at first contact with the water, then she allowed herself to relax back and let the soothing heat seep through her bones. It felt so luxurious. If she stretched out her right arm the limoncello was just within reach. She snagged the glass and sipped a little more for its soothing medicinal properties. As the minutes drifted by and her muscles lost their tension, the horror receded and she floated into a gentle doze-like trance.

Valentino paused with his razor to contemplate his reflection. Above the shaving foam, his angry swollen eye glared back at him. *Sacramento,* he looked like the loser in a prize fight. Unbelievable it was *she* who had inflicted the injury. How did that sweet, feminine little woman come by such a punishing fist?

He regarded himself with rueful amusement. It wasn't all bad. At least after his disastrous lack of control in bedding her she'd be forced to talk to him now. *Grazie a Dio* that for all his sins he hadn't given into his temptation to question her more closely about her cousin.

The results there were mystifying. There was a curious lack of information about Miss Lauren Renfern, apart from her photographic career, as if officialdom had somehow slipped up in its record-keeping. There were some intriguing possibilities he could have suggested, but he still needed to dig deeper.

And against his own judgement, Valentino had found himself digging deeper into Pia's past too. He wasn't sick. It wasn't a case of reaching any particular crossroads.

And it wasn't that he was an especially curious guy. Not usually. But when a woman continually surprised him it was only natural his interest should be piqued. And with her reluctance to reveal the most elementary things about herself, how was he to see the true picture if he didn't run a check?

It didn't have to mean anything significant.

Pia Renfern was different. Too complicated. Too difficult for a straightforward guy like himself. As for this hogswill about her being a free spirit...

He wouldn't believe it. She just wasn't the type.

What did being a free spirit mean anyway? Did she think

she could live any sort of a life without a man? Plenty of women did, of course. But in her case it just didn't ring true.

He'd felt pretty certain he'd find nothing against her.

Still, the wait had been agony and when the email with the priority attachments had finally flashed into his inbox his blood pressure had made a monumental leap and his fingers had needed to brace themselves on the mouse before clicking.

Of course he had been right in his assessment, In Pia's case, Pia's *delicious* case, his instincts were fully borne out. There was one minor traffic infringement, incurred when she was much younger. Regrettable, and no laughing matter, but it didn't surprise him in the slightest with what he knew of her. But apart from her tendency to drive faster than the law allowed, she was a cleanskin.

What really grabbed him, though, and had moved him in some mysterious way, was to learn that she had been a victim of crime. And not only a victim, a *recent* victim.

Why hadn't she mentioned it? Surely something like that would seem huge in the life of the average civilian, especially one so…soft. He was a reasonable guy, wasn't he? Friendly, trustworthy? Sure, there'd been a glitch over his handling of the Fiorello encounter and the sex, but she'd had opportunities where she could have told him. *If* she'd thought he was someone she could rely on. He frowned.

It shouldn't have mattered, but it did. Facts gathered through a database could be fascinating, but they lacked the sheer compelling power of information confided face to face.

Whether she trusted him or not, every decent instinct he had, professional or otherwise, demanded he should warn her and work at extracting her from the unhealthy sphere of La Fiorello. And he would do it for her own good.

Flexing the muscles in his arms and shoulders, he felt an energising surge of masculine satisfaction.

The Renfern case was going well.

Uber well.

All he had to remember was not to succumb to his baser instincts. No flirting, no lusting, no seduction. At least his current disfigurement should work for him in that regard.

Anyway, what sort of a low life would even contemplate having sex with a woman he'd only just plucked from drowning in the sea?

Pia stood on a towelling bath mat to dry herself, wondering what she could put on besides her shorts and top. Her sea-soaked swimsuit lay in an unappealing huddle on the tiles, and, unable to bear the thought of crawling back into it, she resigned herself to going without underwear for a space. This posed the age-old feminine problem. What to do about her nipples?

Six months ago, in another time and place, the true bohemian Pia Renfern might have risked it and sashayed forth free and nonchalant. But here in the Silvestri stronghold? With Valentino oozing testosterone from every gorgeous pore and strutting around his home territory like a sultan?

A sharp knock came on the door and she heard his deep voice, questioning, curious, even a little suspicious. 'Pia? Are you all right?'

Starting, she called hurriedly, 'Yes, yes. I'm fine. I won't be long.'

She dragged on her clothes fast, then made a search through the towel cupboard for some sort of nipple camouflage. Chewing her lip, she considered the feasibility of draping a towel around her shoulders like a cape. If she claimed she was cold... But she remembered how the male mind worked. She'd have to secure the cape in some way that didn't draw his hawk-like gaze to the very spot she was trying to minimise.

A scrap of material hanging over the edge of the cupboard caught her eye, and she reached up and tweaked it down.

It was a runner. The fabric was light, just a strip of some gauzy voile, but it was wide and, she discovered, long enough to arrange around her shoulders and tie in front in a single knot. So long as she kept her eye on the knot, it should work.

She admired the effect in the mirror. It added an almost Regency-style grace to her shorts-and-top ensemble, and encouraged her to swish about with queenly poise like Emma Woodhouse. Pity she had no mascara.

Finally, dry and dressed, her hair combed into place with her fingers, the threat of nipple exposure nullified, she found her way through to the long sitting room where her host awaited.

He was standing with his back to her, looking out across his balcony through a colonnade of arches to the sea.

He too looked freshly bathed, his lean sexy frame exuding clean masculinity in a polo shirt and blue jeans that fitted him to eye-pleasing perfection. A tension in his lean, powerful frame communicated itself to her own expectant nerves and made them tingle with suspense.

Her pulse started to canter along like a nervous little pony.

He swung around, slowly lowering an ice pack he'd been holding to his face, and swept an unsettling glance over her. Warmly unsettling. His eyes, including the one that was half-closed, smouldered with a high-voltage appreciation that made her quite giddy.

'Ah, you look better.' His deep voice was rich with approval. 'Much better. Your lips are rosy again.'

She chose to overlook the reference to her lips. It might have been purely clinical. *Might.*

'What about your poor eye?' she responded in kind. 'Goodness, it looks quite sore.'

He fired her a keenly searching glance from beneath his luxuriant lashes and mumbled, 'Oh, that. It's nothing.' He crossed to her and steered her towards a capacious recliner. 'Here. You shouldn't be standing. Sit here and put your feet up.'

'Thanks. Look, I'm sorry about before,' she said, allowing herself to be gently enveloped in the deeply cushioned comfort. 'I know I didn't thank you properly for rescuing me. I'm very grateful.'

He shrugged and strolled away from her, pensively rubbing his nape, then he spun about abruptly to rake her with a glance. 'Why did you do it?'

'What, go swimming, you mean?'

'Swimming?' He injected the word with so much contempt she started. 'After I warned you,' he exclaimed. 'I told you of the dangers, so why did you risk your life like that? What is it with you? Why do you have to be so—reckless?'

Reckless? *Her?*

Strangely, though, she began to see the truth of that flattering suggestion. Of course she could be reckless. In fact, something about Valentino Silvestri was sending a burst of wild recklessness whooshing through her bloodstream at that very instant. But the accusation in his brilliant dark eyes forced her to a modest denial.

'I wouldn't say I was *reckless*, exactly. The thing was, I didn't think I was risking my life.'

The accusation in his gaze intensified. 'But I warned you.'

Guilt made her assume an airy sort of bravado. 'Well, yes, but I wasn't sure I could believe you.'

'Cosa?' He flung up his hands in incredulity. 'Do I look like a liar?'

'What a question.' She gave a gentle tinkling laugh and fluttered her lashes. 'No, no. You look… Well, you look…' In fact, with his bruised eye he looked darkly, dangerously sexy. She sent him a glance from beneath her lashes. 'How do I know how you look? I wasn't intending to go in far. You should have warned me about the ledge.' She stretched luxuriously and smiled, waggling her foot at him. 'Do you have any more of that limoncello?'

A veiled alertness had been registering in the tilt of his expressive brows, but at that last request they snapped into a frown. 'Are you sure you can handle it? It *is* forty per cent proof.'

'Of course I can. What a question. Don't you think we have wine in Australia?'

His good eye glinted. He hesitated, then after a moment strolled to a sideboard where the bottle was housed, poured her a less than minuscule drop of the magical stuff and brought it back.

He handed it to her with a veiled expression. 'Sip slowly now,' he commanded in his velvet voice. *'Piano, piano.'*

She held the glass level with her eye. 'You're very generous.'

'It's very strong,' he said drily. 'It should have been brandy, but I've been away so long and...' He shrugged. 'Nonno doesn't keep much here for entertaining. Food is what you should be having now. First, though, I think we must patch your wound.'

Pia savoured a drop on her tongue, and as Valentino Silvestri bore down on her with bandages, firm purpose in his battered face, all at once she felt the full vulnerable force of being naked under her clothes.

Oh, Lord. Here she was again, on the trapeze without a safety net. She should get up right now and walk home. No. *Run.*

'Now,' he said, taking a bottle from a small kit and moistening a piece of cotton wool with its contents. 'This might sting a little, but you're brave, aren't you, Pia?'

Holding the cotton wool poised, he gave her a faintly mocking smile, but it was without malice. His bruised eye gave him a rakish appearance, like some Neapolitan villain. Blame the limoncello, or the aftermath of a traumatic experience, but her wanton flesh longed for him to touch her, even with antiseptic. Even the lightest, slightest brush of those supple fingers.

She moistened her lips. 'I think you know how brave I am.'

He lowered his lashes, and she saw them silhouetted against his cheek. Long, thick and luxuriant. 'I know you can be angry.'

'Anger isn't always such a bad thing, though, is it? It can be quite positive. And healthy, don't you think?'

He smiled to himself, and she watched him dab the graze with cotton wool. Each time he brushed her with his fingers her skin cells shivered with delight. 'You are one healthy woman.'

She allowed that to pass by to the keeper. Her doctor would have been over the moon to see the angry version of Pia Renfern. And Valentino was taking such care with her scrape, applying a bandage and neatly taping it, she was in no mood to quibble.

'Where's your grandfather today?' she enquired breathlessly.

'He went out with the fishermen on the early tide. He likes to see the catch.' His mouth edged up at the corners in wry amusement. 'He hasn't discovered yet he's an old man. They're not likely to come back for hours.'

He glanced up and met her mesmerised gaze.

She felt the atmosphere tauten and her heart started to gallop. She had one of those moments when everything became crystal clear, images, sounds, the mingled scents of antiseptic, lemons and Valentino's lean chiselled face.

He stood up and replaced the cap on the bottle, and stood angled slightly away from her, a tension in his stance.

'Before anything else, I feel I should apologise for referring to your—your difficulty with the *Nastro Azzurro* the other day. That wasn't very—honourable of me.' He met her eyes. 'I understand why you were angry.'

Her heart glowed with a fierce rush of grateful warmth. 'Oh. Fine. Thanks. Apology accepted.' It was such a *relief* to have the opportunity to forgive him.

For that, at least.

The vibrations on the airwaves were exhilarating, but he said nothing more. Nothing that would encourage her to believe he might want to reopen negotiations in the romance department. Yet here she was, feeling so warm and positive towards him, so attracted, so practically aroused she was panting.

She came to the reluctant conclusion that if he didn't say *something*, she would have no option but to drag herself away. Otherwise she might start flirting again and behaving in a way she would later regret.

It was a pity. Now her desire was back hot and strong, what a waste.

She said huskily, 'I—I should probably be going now. Thanks for the antiseptic and everything.' She made a move to get up, but her head made a woozy little lurch and she sank back into the chair.

Looking thunderous, Valentino flung up an autocratic hand. '*Per carita*. You aren't going anywhere. After your ordeal, and all those limoncelli, you need to eat. And as well…' His black lashes screened his eyes. 'There are things you and I need to talk about. Important th—' He glanced at her once, then again, his dark gaze suddenly scorching hot.

She followed the direction of his eyes and her nerve jumped. *Heavens*. The voile was askew, her taut nipples clearly apparent through the fabric of her top. She made to snatch the runner into position but Valentino was there first.

Swiftly he swooped and adjusted it to cover her. 'There, now. See? You're cold. Here…'

He reached for a throw draped over a nearby sofa and tucked it around her, smiling to himself while a chaos of sensations went to war in her. She closed her eyes, intoxicated by his spicy masculine scent, her nerve endings aquiver where his fingers brushed her and his clean-shaven jaw almost grazed her cheek.

'Now,' he said, his dark *cioccolato* voice deepening to a purr. 'We'll see how we can warm you up.' He straightened, and as he strode away ordered, 'Don't move from that spot.'

What was she doing? She was no invalid. She should get up, walk home and make her own breakfast. He clearly wanted her to stay, and why? She wasn't naive enough to think it was because he was concerned about the state of her health.

But...

It was lovely here with stripes of sunlight on the tiles and, anyway, he needed to talk to her. How churlish of her would it be to bite the very desirable hand extending the olive branch, so to speak?

She'd stay just a little while. She wouldn't allow herself to become too cosy. She'd firmly resist the fogging of her brain, and anyway, her limbs felt heavy and pleasant.

The throw was soft and sensual on her skin. She dragged it up to her chin and surrendered to the warm fuzzy glow, wrapped in a delicious languour.

In the kitchen, Valentino pressed a frozen pack to his throbbing eye and leaned back against the bench while he waited for the coffee machine. He drew a long breath.

Miss Pia Renfern fresh from a bath, stretching her lovely limbs like a cat, her cheek soft and fragrant, her hair silky clean, made his mouth water. Added to that was the stimulating knowledge that, however cleverly she might have tried to conceal it, underneath those clothes her slim, shapely body was completely without underwear.

He felt himself harden.

With a vision in his mind's eye of rose-tipped nipples and soft blonde curls, he frothed some milk for the coffees, then piled bread and pastries from the bakery boy's basket onto a tray with plates and tossed on a couple of napkins he found in a drawer.

But... He must not be carried away. He was a professional guy. Steel when the occasion demanded. The Renfern case needed to be kept under control.

* * *

'Hungry?'

Pia stirred from her little drift, stretched voluptuously under her blanket and smiled. Hungry? Call her ravenous.

Valentino set the tray down on a coffee table, and she bestirred herself from her recliner and joined him on the sofa, her blanket wrapped around her and tucked in at her breast.

She surveyed the small feast eagerly. There was bread, crusty white as well as olive flavoured, a little prosciutto, some cherry tomatoes, and croissants still warm from the oven. 'This is lovely. I'm utterly famished.' She accepted a frothy cappucino. 'Do you always take such good care of people you fish out of the sea?'

'If they're *bella*. If they're *dolce*.' The corners of his mouth edged up, his gleaming gaze on her face, her throat.

'Oh, *bella*,' she scoffed, though she felt herself go slightly pink while her dizzy pulse quickened. 'You need to get your eyes checked. And I'm not always sweet.'

He looked grave. 'The sweetness is only good when it is tempered with the tartness. Too much sweetness can be—*molto troppo*. This is why I like a woman who can be angry, who can be fierce, then in another minute she is *appassionata*, like a tempest, and still so—so *soave* in her touch.'

She couldn't help laughing. 'Oh, you're such a shameless flatterer. I think I know who is *soave*.' She pulled a croissant open with her fingers and spread it with jam. 'What's this?'

'Marmellata di ciliegi.'

'Is that cherry? Ah, yes, I *love* cherry.' She spread her croissant and took a sumptuous bite, savouring it while he watched. In a couple more bites she finished it off, washed it down with coffee, then licked her fingers with voluptuous enjoyment.

Smiling through her lashes, she met his hot, intent gaze. 'Go on, then. Thrill me. Say it again.'

He obliged with a stream of lilting Italiano, which she guessed by his lascivious expression had little to do with cherry jam, though she dared not ask *what*, then he picked up her napkin, leaned close and touched it to her upper lip. 'You have a little froth just here.'

'Oh.' As she parted her lips to speak he took her face in his hands and kissed her. Her heart bounced in her chest, then settled into a thrilled racing while her lips, her nipples, the blood thundering through her veins all warmed to the fantastic friction of Valentino tasting each of her lips separately and sliding them through his teeth in a slow, erotic burn.

Her insides melted into a puddle and her brain shut down due to foggy conditions.

'I think we must remove this blanket,' he murmured, unhooking it from her bodice, then he slipped his hands under it until it fell away.

She didn't mind. She was far too hot for it anyway. Especially when he untied her gauzy runner, revealing the points of her nipples in all their aroused glory, then tenderly teased them and stroked her breasts, sending amazing thrills tingling through every tiny nerve and making them swell with the intense and erotic pleasure.

For some reason her flesh felt extra sensitive to touch this sunlit morning, and every caress sent electric ripples shooting through her skin like meteoric sparks. A few arousing minutes of his sexy, questing lips on her throat, his hands exploring under her clothes, and she was in passion's grip, her entire being ablaze with desire.

He drew away from her, a deeply sexual flame in the depths of his darkened eyes that aroused a hungry, breathless anticipation inside her.

'Come,' he said, rising and holding out his hand.

She took the hand, willing to follow him anywhere at that moment, but, true to thrilling form, with a triumphant laugh he swiftly swept her up into his arms.

While she might have teased him for his caveman instincts, in truth being rushed to his bed was a delicious excitement. And on this occasion she was utterly alive to being held against his lean angular body, the strong beat of his heart, the promise of his erection nudging her hip.

He carried her up the stairs and into a white, sparsely furnished room with windows open to the sea, kicking the door shut behind him with his foot.

He didn't drop her quite as unceremoniously onto his wide bed as he had on hers. Rather he deposited her carefully, stripping away the covers first and ensuring her head landed gently on his pillow.

Still, even if he was intending to take it more slowly this time, he didn't waste a second in stripping off, and she had an uninterrupted view of his big powerful body, the wide chest, lean waist and hips, long bronzed thighs that so thrilled her. The sight of his jutting penis sent a pang of raw, trembling excitement sizzling through her nerve fibres.

'Oh,' she exclaimed, moistening her dry lips. 'Hurry.'

'Hurry?' He sat on the bed, assessing the nature of her arousal with a quizzical examination of her face. 'Are you sure? You've been through a physical ordeal.'

'I'm going through a physical ordeal right now,' she said throatily and ran her finger down his arm, into the underside of his forearm where sinews stretched with devastating masculine appeal. She sensed the tremor of response under his satin skin, saw the flare in his eyes.

'I'll do what I can,' he growled.

She sat up and removed her top, then surrendered herself while his smooth, lean hands unbuttoned her shorts, drew down the zip, then slipped them down and off.

His hot, hungry gaze devoured her nakedness. *'Bella,'* he said, his voice deep, trembling a little, roughened by desire. 'You are *bellissima*. You are all I think about. At night, in the morning, when I am waking, when I am sleeping.'

A thrill galvanised her heart. 'And you are all *I* think about,' she said shakily.

His dark eyes were fiercely tender. 'I can't let you be hurt again. Never again.'

She blinked. For a wild minute the bank incident flashed through her mind, though of course that had nothing to do with anything here. Another life, another country.

'Well, I'll try not to be,' she said, trembling to her excited core.

Lying alongside her, he gripped her arms, his eyes so burningly aroused her insides thrilled. 'Now, *tesoro*. Tell me what it is you like.'

Unused to such a request, she actually flushed. 'Well...I like being stroked—softly, and, you know—*warmly*, all over.' As she warmed to the theme her lashes wanted to fall halfway, and her voice grew sultry as if she were taken over by some languid temptress. She drawled her words with voluptuous sensuality. 'I like you to touch me. My face, my hair, my ears, my chest, my—back, my legs, and here...' She indicated her pelvic region. '*And*—and what I *really* like,' she placed a hand on his bicep and said huskily, 'is the feel of you inside me.'

'Ah.' With every word she'd uttered his eyes had become darker and more inflamed until they were smouldering hot coals. And unless she was imagining what she was seeing, his proud erection had grown even more majestic.

'*Molto bene,*' he growled, his sensuous mouth edging up at the corners. 'But first we will go gently.'

'*Fantastico.*' She smiled through her lashes. '*Piano, piano.*'

Softly, tenderly, he stroked her all over, with lips as well as fingers, trailing fire in every corner of her purring being, then he parted her thighs, and stroked the folds of her sex with a soft, soft hand, finding, to her intense pleasure, the sensitive nub of her clitoris.

To her voluptuous delight, he positioned himself between her legs and kissed the places his fingers had previously caressed, and allowed his tongue to softly, thrillingly, penetrate inside her and tickle the yearning satin walls.

The sensation was so sexy she writhed, she whimpered, she moaned in rapture.

Suddenly in a rapid tumultuous rush her orgasm blossomed inside her and dissolved like a sunburst, irradiating her with an intense and satisfying release.

Strangely, her appetite to proceed was barely diminished. Perhaps because Valentino, lounging in satisfaction of a gift well delivered, his black lashes at half mast like some smouldering, slumberous panther with one black eye, was a temptation too delicious for any red-blooded woman to withstand for long, she gave him little time to rest.

She assisted him in donning a condom, then straddled him and gently, tenderly, eased herself onto him, and had the intense excitement of sliding up and down that rock-hard shaft until she was filled to the brim with ecstasy and their passion soared to shattering climaxes.

And that was only the start. Valentino had much to teach her that she hadn't known before, especially about gentleness and the sheer erotic turn-on of masculine tenderness and consideration.

They only lifted their heads when clattering from below reminded Valentino the cleaning woman had arrived, and he poked his head out of the door and issued an executive command that she only bother with the lower level that day, and stay away from the upper.

In fact, Pia might have stayed locked in his arms in a state of impassioned bliss all day long if their pleasure hadn't been interrupted at last by the sounds of doors opening and closing, a radio, and an elderly voice calling, *'Tino, Tino, dove sei?'*

CHAPTER ELEVEN

'THAT'S Nonno.'

With one accord Valentino and Pia scrambled up, dived for their clothes and each made a rush for the en-suite bathroom, crashing into each other at the door.

'You go first.'

'No, you go. Don't panic, I'll talk to him.'

Pia didn't linger long in Valentino's bathroom. She had a hasty all-over wash, including her glowing face with its puffy, swollen, kiss-ravaged lips, then hastily dressed in what she had, while Valentino took his turn to wash and dragged on his jeans and shirt.

'Is there another exit?' she breathed, horrified to be caught *in flagrante delicto*, so to speak.

He nodded. 'Downstairs. Don't worry. He'll be starting the cooking. He won't even see you.'

'Oh, but...' Aghast, she realised her precious runner was still downstairs on the sofa. 'Would you mind going down first and bringing up my runner?'

She explained, and, amused, Valentino complied, strolling down to the sitting room only to find that all evidence of the breakfast excitements had been cleared by the indefatigable Mirella.

Enzio caught sight of him and came bustling from the kitchen with tales of the morning's catch, and was brought up short by the sight of Valentino's developing bruise. '*Mamma mia*, what has happened to you?'

'What? Oh, this. I bumped into something. Not to worry, it's nothing. How was the voyage?'

'Not bad. Some lobster, squid, a little bass.' The old man peered closely at him. 'You need a chunk of meat to put on there. What was it?'

'Something near the rocks. Where I was swimming.' Valentino met the shrewd eyes and held them firmly.

Enzio's brows elevated but he said nothing more about the curious wound. 'So.' He rubbed his hands. 'Mirella has started the soup, the fish are ready for cooking, and you can collect the vegetables from the garden, if you can *see* well enough. Only wait while I wash off all these fish scales and change my clothes.'

He could see well enough, Valentino reflected. He'd seen treasures aplenty this morning. That reminded him of the need to hunt for something strategic for Pia to wear. He came upon her swimsuit hanging in the laundry, apparently having been washed and now dried by the warm air. His brows knitted. Whatever Mirella made of a woman's swimsuit in one of the Silvestri bathrooms would be old news in Positano by the time he next made it to the *piazza*.

It would be a pity if the town gossips got wind of his affair, and experience had taught him they would be especially hard on Pia.

He carried the swimsuit upstairs.

A savoury aroma of cooking wafted to Pia as she walked down to the front entrance with Valentino, at least looking respectable. Whatever it was smelled rich, herbal and delicious, provoking hunger pangs of a different sort from those she'd recently been assuaging. She'd just turned for a hasty farewell on the doorstep when an elderly figure appeared in the hall behind Valentino, a query on his lips.

She swiftly pulled away from Valentino, and came face to

face with the old man she'd seen working in the garden most mornings. His was a remarkable face. The creases of age had settled into lines of humour and sadness, strength and wisdom. Sharp brown eyes, bright with curiosity, scrutinised her from head to toe.

Valentino took charge.

'Nonno,' he said in English. 'This is Pia Renfern, our neighbour. Pia—Enzio Silvestri, my grandpapa.'

'Aha.' The old man's brows were lifted high. 'Our *neighbour*.' He managed to inject the word with both surprise and comprehension, as if her being a neighbour explained everything. Like what she was doing kissing his grandson on the doorstep. Had he noticed their embrace? Pia wondered. Could she possibly pretend she'd dropped by for a cup of sugar?

'*Signore,*' Pia said, extending her hand. He accepted it in his gnarled old hand and with grave courtesy leaned forward to brush each of her cheeks with his.

'Pia, you say. Where then are you living?'

She pointed up the hill and explained about Lauren's apartment.

'*Sì.*' The old man nodded, registering every item of information with care. 'I know it. Maybe I have seen her, your cousin. She has the long hair?'

'Yes, that would be Lauren. Really long brown hair.'

Enzio smiled, his shrewd gaze switching between her and Valentino, surmise in his eyes. Was the secret passion pulsing between them and making the air sing apparent to other people? Pia wondered.

'Tino, you should invite your guest. Pia, you will please dine with us.'

Pia hesitated, her glance flying to Valentino. Her instinct was to decline and flee. With the sheets still piping hot, so to speak, the presence of a third party could be fraught with awkwardness. As well, Valentino's eyes had veiled and his body language suggested a definite reluctance.

Everything between them was too raw, too sweet and wild for family members to witness.

'That's very kind, *signore*,' she said quickly, 'but I mustn't intrude. I just met Valentino swimming a bit earlier and dropped by for a—a chat.' She barely blushed. 'I really should be at home, er—working.'

'Ah, *swimming*,' the grandfather said. 'So you have been swimming?' He nodded long and meditatively. *'Sì, sì, sì, sì, sì.'*

Pia noticed a glance pass between them, stern on Valentino's side, solemn on his grandfather's. Valentino murmured something to him in Italian, and Enzio argued back with vigour.

In the end Valentino patted his shoulder with an amused grimace and turned to Pia. 'He begs you. We would be greatly honoured if you would eat with us in one hour.' His eyes twinkled. 'He wants me to assure you we are very fine cooks and the fish will never be as sweet as they are at this moment in the history of the universe.'

There was nothing for it but to give in and accept gracefully. At least she would have an hour to compose herself. She should be able to keep her hands off Valentino for the course of a meal. Surely.

Her body still humming with the aftermath of love, she walked home and soaked in a long refreshing shower. Then she put on a sundress, sandals and a little make-up.

It was never the Australian way to arrive as a guest empty-handed, so, searching for something she could take as a contribution, she decided on the wine Lola had brought.

And truly it was lovely, being ushered into the Silvestri inner sanctum. Valentino greeted her at the door and escorted her inside to where his grandfather was waiting. Enzio kissed her as if they hadn't exchanged greetings only an hour earlier, and accepted her gift with warm approval.

'Can I do anything to help?' she enquired. 'I'd be very happy to help with the salad. Wash the lettuce, if you'd like.'

Neither of them would hear of it, to her regret.

At first the old gentleman ensconced her royally in the sitting room with great solemnity, a glass of crisp white wine and a platter of bread and olives.

She sat there a while hugging herself with amazement over the day's events so far. An Italian lover. She had a bone fide, certified Italian *lover*. How had she, Pia Renfern, managed it? The most tender, virile, sexy, *gorgeous* Italian lover.

Lunch was served in a rather formal dining room she suspected was rarely used. There were starched antimacassars on the chair backs, and wedding photos on the wall, of both a very young Enzio and his bride, and Valentino's parents, also looking ridiculously young by modern standards.

More family pictures adorned a side table with a lace cloth, and she wished she could examine them all more closely. From where she sat, she could make out a younger Valentino, looking devastating in uniform.

The meal began with a delicious vegetable soup. It was followed by a dish of mussels, another of eggplant roasted with herbs and parmesan, and whole fish fried in olive oil with a piquant lemon and caper sauce. The salad came last, lettuce leaves included. After Valentino served her with a generous helping, she made a surreptitious inspection but could detect no life-threatening organisms, none visible to the naked eye, at least.

Though Enzio did most of the talking, she had the sense Valentino was in control. Valentino served the food and took care of the changeover between courses. The old man deferred to him often, and there was a soft note in Valentino's voice whenever he addressed his grandfather, as if he was taking care to be gentle.

Enzio, on the other hand, only had eyes for Pia. Everything she said, everything she *did* seemed to charm him as if she were a visiting princess from some enchanted royal line.

'Do you cook, Pia?' he enquired.

'I try,' she admitted, smiling. 'I wouldn't dare claim it *here*, though. I can just about rustle up a good Thai stir-fry.'

Enzio looked mystified and appealed to Valentino for clarification. 'Ah.' He nodded when Valentino explained. 'A Thai stir-fry.' His brow furrowed. 'This Thai stir-fry might be very *good…*' though it was clear from his expression that he thought it unlikely '…but the best food, the very best of all, is Italiano. And of the Italiano, the cooking of Campania is very fine. How many weeks do you stay with us?'

'Four or five. We'll see how it goes.' She felt a twinge to have to acknowledge that her visit was finite. How would it be when Valentino's few days were up and he was gone? What would she do then? Her sunshine was on borrowed time. She suppressed a surge of panic.

From across the table she felt Valentino's intelligent gaze on her, curious and assessing, and lowered hers. If he had the slightest inkling of how she felt, how quickly he'd be on that white stallion galloping for the horizon.

'Not much time for you to learn,' Enzio said worriedly. 'Tino, we will have to work fast.'

With a laugh Valentino said, 'Nonno, Pia has a mother at home in Australia to teach her cooking.'

'Is she Italiano?' Enzio said.

'No, I'm afraid not,' Pia confessed, smiling. 'But Australians adore Italian food. I'm sure every household in Australia makes lasagne.'

The corrugations in Enzio's brow multiplied. *'Lasagne.'*

His horror at the Australian version of lasagne was so apparent Pia had to laugh. Still, underneath her laughter the realisation was forced upon her that Valentino was in no way so caught up in the magic he was forgetful of reality. His imminent departure and her eventual one were right up there in his frontal lobes. While for her, the sweeter every moment now, the more bitter would be the separation to come.

But for the moment she was in love, she was with friends,

the food tasted wonderful, and she wanted to extract every atom of happiness from being enveloped in such warmth. More than that, her lover was charming and attentive, teasing her with wickedness where Enzio's facility with English did not extend.

Unable to touch, they had to satisfy themselves with looking. Every dark, slumberous glance from Valentino only whetted her appetite for the next time she would be alone with him.

The day had felt close to perfect. She felt enveloped in warmth, with Enzio so kind and funny, making jokes and laughing. When the glasses were refilled he congratulated her on the wine she had brought. 'A very fine wine from Capri,' he said, beaming. 'You choose like an Italiana.'

'Thank you, *signore*, but I can't claim to have chosen it,' she confessed. 'It was given to me by a friend who lives there.'

'Ah.' His eyes widened. 'You have some friends on Capri?'

'Not exactly. They're really my cousin's friends. I've only met Lola the one time. Lola Fiorello. Her husband is the movie director.'

A strange expression entered Enzio's gaze. His smile was wiped from his face and he cast a swift glance at Valentino. 'Fiorello? She was the woman, the friend of Ariana?'

Valentino hesitated, then spoke to his grandfather in rapid Italian. When Enzio replied with a veiled glance at Pia, Valentino placed his hand on his arm as though to restrain him, speaking in tones of urgent persuasion.

'Who's Ariana?' Pia said.

There was a moment of silence, then both Silvestris spoke simultaneously.

'Valentino's wife.'

'My ex-wife.'

Pia absorbed the information, only her suffering heartbeat attesting to the shock gathering itself for a heavier onslaught later, when she would be alone.

The old gentleman looked from Valentino's face to hers and

back again, then gently replaced his napkin. He turned towards Pia. '*Signorina*. It has been very pleasant to make your acquaintance.' Stiffly he rose from the table. He looked pale and all at once fragile, a slight jerkiness in his movements. '*Scusi*, I am finding I am a little tired. *Buona sera*, Pia, Tino.'

Looking after him with a concerned expression, Valentino suddenly sprang to his feet and followed his grandfather from the room. '*Nonno.*'

Pia was left sitting amongst the wreckage, waiting, but Valentino didn't return. After thirty or so minutes of mounting confusion and concern she cleared the dishes and carried them to the kitchen.

How many opportunities had she given him to reveal his former marriage? Even on the very first day he could have told her the truth. And why didn't he come back to talk about it? What sort of a man couldn't face a woman with the truth? A man still in love with his wife?

She did a little rinsing and tidying, but, unsure of the protocols with leftovers, unsure of anything on earth, decided not to go any further with cleaning up.

With a leaden heart she let herself out of the front door and walked home. Ran, actually.

CHAPTER TWELVE

AFTER the earliest night in years, Pia had just fallen into a dream where she was easily able to fly in a vertical position, though it still felt terrifying to be looking down on the tree tops, when a ringing sound penetrated the mists and pulled her back down to her bed and into her body. Eventually she woke to the realisation that she was in Italy, it was the middle of the night and someone was ringing the doorbell.

As she adjusted to full consciousness, the hurt feeling she had every time she thought of Valentino revived with renewed force.

She reached for the lamp and was amazed to discover it was still only nine-thirty. Stumbling from the bed, she threw her pashmina around her shoulders and bumped her way to the front door. Her hand faltered on the knob. Who was it likely to be? Would a serial killer ring the bell?

'Who is it?' she croaked.

'Valentino.'

She opened the door and blinked at him. He looked grim and purposeful in black jeans and a thin black sweater, his shadowed jaw stern, a serious glitter in his dark, semi-bruised gaze. He swept a glance over her and just for an instant a flame flared in his eyes.

After a second or two he said silkily, 'Am I to be invited in?'

She moved aside. He strode past smelling of the night and

the sea, then turned back and pulled her to him, kissing her lips, her throat. She could feel the electricity of his lean body, his strong heart drumming against hers with a vibrant pulse that even in such confusing circumstances compelled a leap of excitement in her veins.

With an effort of will she disengaged herself. First things first.

In the sitting room she faced him. 'How is your grandfather? Is he all right? Was it because of me that he...?'

He shrugged and spread his hands. 'No, no. He's fine. Sleeping. You know he is in his eighties. He's been doing too many things today.' He glanced at her, then dropped his lashes. 'I'm sorry you were—left alone.'

She shrugged a casual dismissal.

It was a moment when he might have taken her in his arms, but she forestalled that by knotting her pashmina more securely and retreating elegantly to one of the armchairs. The damage was done, anyway. Now she had the imprint of his lips on her mouth and throat, her skin burned for another taste.

After a second Valentino succumbed to the signals and took the sofa. He leaned forward, elbows resting on his thighs, hands clasped, staring at the rug, his handsome face unreadable.

'Nonno had a little moment of weakness while you were there this afternoon,' he explained. 'I didn't like to leave him.'

Pia exclaimed in concern. 'Oh, no.'

'Don't worry. He's fine now. But I didn't intend to leave you there for so long. All alone and wondering. I came back to talk to you about it but you were gone.' He gave her a keen glance, his dark eyes shrewd.

For a second she wished she were a seventies porn star, and could drag out a languid cigarette, light up, and exhale a poisonous cloud. At any rate, she crossed her legs. Pity she was in her nightie and had no five inch heels to accentuate their shapeliness.

'About...?

He scratched his ear. 'Perhaps you are thinking I should have mentioned my marriage.'

'Why would I think that?'

His eyes glinted. 'Exactly. Why would you?'

'You owe me nothing, after all. The past is past.'

'And it's not as if I have lied to you.' He lilted his spectacular brows, threw out his hands.

'Unless, of course, you call it a lie of *omission*.' She watched his face and he smiled, meeting her gaze without apparent shame.

'I have no doubt we are all guilty of keeping things to ourselves, *cara mia*. Even when we find ourselves opening to the possibilities of connecting with someone who excites us.'

A certain warmth crept into her cheeks, but she said rather loftily, 'If you're referring to my being a painter, there were reasons I didn't want to discuss my work.'

His eyes gleamed. 'Ah. The temperament of the artist must be taken into account.'

A small silence fell. She certainly didn't feel the need to open that can of worms. The painting block led straight to the stress disorder, the stress disorder was the high road to the bank incident, the bank incident led to head shrinkers and the supposition in minds like Euan's she was a weak, loopy, unreliable mental case.

She cleared her throat. 'I suppose your divorce was quite recent.'

He lifted his shoulders. 'Five years.'

'Five?' She was surprised, and relieved. 'Oh. Well, you seemed so angry with Lola, frothing with rage like the red hot lava of Vesuvius, I thought it must be more recent. I've even been wondering if she was involved in some way. If you and *she*—'

With a thunderstruck expression he said, '*No*. Wipe that from your mind.' He punched his fist into his palm and accompanied it with a stream of emphatic and very convincing

Italiano. '*Nothing* like that. What happened in the past was—
complicated. But…' he lifted his hands in rueful resignation
'…it was a divorce. What divorce isn't? I didn't care to mention it to you because…' He hesitated, his jaw clenching, and
it was as though the words were forcibly extracted through his
gritted teeth. 'I am not proud of these events.'

'You were wounded,' she surmised softly.

Frowning, he flashed her a non-committal glance and waggled his lean hand. '*Cosi cosi.* I… Soon after our marriage I
was called away to sea for many months. Ariana grew bored
and spent a great deal of time over at the Villa Fiorello.' He
gave a wry shrug. 'The truth was, she found she didn't like
being married to an old-fashioned navy *carabiniere* as much
as she enjoyed playing sophisticated games with celebrities.'

He looked so grim, with such distaste in his expression,
Pia's imagination ran riot. What sort of games? Celebrity strip-
teases? Pole dancing? Wild orgies with drug-crazed movie di-
rectors? Sleazy politicians?

'Stories leaked out, as they always will, and there was a na-
tionwide scandal. It was in the media for weeks. My wife's picture was on the front page of every European newsrag, along
with—some famous terrible people.' He grimaced and made
what could have been a shudder. 'In the end— Well, now she
has an acting career. Have you heard of her? Ariana da Silva?'

Pia shook her head. 'Sorry.'

His face was impassive. 'You will. I believe she's considered a big talent.' His lip curled. 'Being married to me would
have smothered her creativity, so Lola said. She's married now
to this Argentinian film guy.'

His sensuous mouth widened, but it was barely a smile,
shadowed as it was with the bitterness of remembered anguish.

The depth of Pia's dismay rendered her speechless. Her
heart went out to him. She had a strong inkling he'd mini-
mised the extent of it and barely revealed a hint of the ordeal
he'd endured. The disgrace. His soul excoriated with shame.

His control of his proud, stern face, so dignified, so beautiful, touched a deep emotional chord in her.

'I'm so sorry,' she said, tears blurring her eyes. 'You must have gone through a terrible time. It must have been—devastating.'

He made a minimal acknowledgement with his hands and shoulders. 'It was hardest for Nonno, living here and facing his friends in the village every day. You saw today... He still finds it painful to be reminded. In my case...' He shrugged. 'I resigned my position and found other work. Now *Grazie a Dio* the—the episode is—in the past and we can all move on.'

Oh, God. He'd lost his job over it. His *career*. She gazed searchingly at him, wondering if he'd sought any counselling. She knew too well how it felt, carrying a load of shame and a loss of public face, though it was hard to imagine someone with his powerful chest and lean, iron-hard frame being anything but impervious.

The understanding crystallised in her as never before that underneath that powerful exterior there was a big, strong heart beating. A heart that could suffer. And *had*.

She felt a rush of such intense warmth for him. If only she could find a way to heal that damaged heart, she'd do it. She'd move mountains. She'd...

She flew across to the sofa and hugged him, showering his face with kisses.

'I'm so glad you have that positive attitude,' she said, warmly stroking him, grateful to have had at least enough experience herself to be able to offer some sage words, however small. 'After a trauma like that it takes time, but it's best to let go of your negative feelings. And I really appreciate you telling me all this. Honestly.'

He smiled, holding her close. 'Life goes on.'

'It does.'

He continued to scan her face, his brows a little elevated, eyes glinting, then he got up from the sofa and started to pace, a few steps one way, then a few steps back. He said stiffly, 'This is—not something I reveal to people, usually.'

'Of *course* not. I'm honoured that you've...trusted me with your—personal experience.'

'I would hope that you and I could find some ground to trust each other, Pia.' He halted and looked keenly at her. He added softly, 'If we are to be true lovers.'

What? Her heartbeat bounded in joyful shock.

He seized her hands and pulled her up. 'Is it possible, *tesoro*? Can we be together for a time?'

She put her arms around his neck and answered him with a kiss. True lovers. How she adored those words. If Euan had ever thought of saying anything like that...

He paused from kissing her to say, 'No doubt there are things you've experienced in your life as well, *amore*. Things you'd like to share.'

Desire was humming through her, lighting her up like fireworks, and she could feel its answering throb in his big, vibrant body, binding her to him like an irresistible cord.

'Oh, nothing like that,' she breathed. 'Nothing so—life-shattering.'

He gazed quizzically at her, a slight frown between his eyes. 'Nothing?'

Well, there was the bank incident of course, but she could hardly be expected to tell him that, with all the likely fallout. Did she want to put him off? Anyway, it was nowhere near what he'd suffered with the divorce.

He released her after a second, and still with that small frown made a move towards the door.

Taken aback, she gasped, 'You're leaving?'

He paused with his back to her. There was a tension in the set of his wide shoulders. 'It's been a long day. I think—maybe we should both get some sleep.'

'Oh, but...' She wasn't exactly pleading, but her sudden removal from his arms was a massive let-down, like being cast into outer darkness. She threw out her hands in confusion, and her pashmina slid to the floor.

'Maybe we both need to reflect.' He threw her a glance, and then as though magnetically drawn his gaze swivelled back for another. A hot gleam lit his eyes. 'Perhaps we need to think... think about what we really... You are looking quite chaste in that nightdress.'

'*Chaste?*'

Honestly, she was astounded, and the tiniest bit offended. Wasn't she a bona fide red-hot mamma? Admittedly her nightie was white, with lace, pintucks and tiny blue forget-me-nots embroidered around the bodice, but the fabric was very fine. Not see-through exactly, except in certain lights, but the deep bodice was quite flattering to her cleavage and the gown did have a tendency to skim her shape as she moved.

'*Sì.*' His lashes flickered down and his voice softened. 'You are reminding me of a virgin, *una bella vergine desiderabile.*'

There was something deeply arousing about those words, or maybe it was the way he curled them around his tongue. Call it a contradiction in terms, but somehow they triggered a sense of challenge in her. How many men had ever described her as looking like a beautiful, desirable virgin? He was making her *feel* beautiful and desirable, all curves and breasts and soft, pliant femininity, tingling, *yearning* to be touched.

But what was the point if he walked out of the door?

She drew a breath. 'You know, it's funny you should say that, Valentino. I *feel* like a virgin.'

His strong brows lifted and the gleam in his eyes grew piercing. 'After this morning?'

'I know.' The old throaty voice was beginning to overtake her. 'Amazing, isn't it? But I've bathed so often today I feel all soft...and fragrant...and sweetly, sweetly virginal.' She injected so much sensuality into the words they even convinced *her*. '*Feel* me. I'm trembling.' She brushed his bronzed arm with hers, and he quivered as if from a bolt of electricity. She said solemnly, 'I feel like some mediaeval princess who's been locked in a tower for twenty-six years. As if—as if no man must ever touch me.'

His eyes sharpened and flickered to her breasts. '*No* man?'

She lowered her lashes. 'Well, I suppose… If there was one who was especially virile…'

He laughed, then all at once he dragged her so close to him their pelvises touched and his chest was grazing her nipples through the cloth.

'I think I can promise you something pretty exceptional,' he said thickly, encouraging her with the virile bulge she detected beneath his belt buckle. Then, like the wild animal he was, for the third time since morning he dragged her triumphantly to the nearest available lair.

It was a night of highs and lows, so to speak, with desire giving way to passion and passion surrendering to sleep in the hour before dawn. But before the cock crowed three times her lover was up and dragging on his clothes.

'I have to check on Nonno,' he told Pia when she lifted her tousled head. 'He wakes early and I want to be there.' He kissed her. 'Keep my pillow warm.'

Then he was gone.

Something was gnawing at her. She had much to think about, and she was feeling a little fatigued, so she slept in, had a leisurely shower, an even more leisurely breakfast, and chose to spend what was left of the morning working on her landscape.

A scrutiny of the watercolour persuaded her it wasn't completely hopeless, but it was time for a more passionate rendering in oils.

She tried to concentrate on the positives while she was slapping on the colour, the pleasures, all the beautiful moments with Valentino. But try as she might to cling to the rose-coloured world, there were shadows lurking around the edges. Something he'd said last night.

Together for a time. How long was a time?

When he'd first said it she'd blithely assumed he'd meant for the few days he was in town. That would fit in perfectly with her new paradigm, after all. Love 'em and leave 'em Renfern. Maybe he would consider flying back to see her from time to time once he went back to work.

She laid down her brush and rested her head in her hands. Oh, please. How much of a fraud was she? The truth was, she couldn't face the thought of the goodbye. Losing him was unthinkable. It would tear her heart out. She closed her eyes. Oh, how she needed to make the most of what time she had, for Lauren would come back one day and...

Seeking sustenance from the sea, Valentino plotted a course for Ischia and headed across the Bay. He needed to think, and where better to do it than the scenes of his disillusionment? Ischia, Capri... Playgrounds of the wealthy, both legitimately and otherwise.

In his mind the shadow of the Fiorellos and their circle of friends hung over the islands like a curse. He'd always had hopes of pinning something on them to avenge a tiny piece of his trampled honour. Why else had he joined Interpol? There was little doubt, with the Fiorello millions far exceeding their apparent income, a successful operation could be mounted there.

If his staff weren't overloaded with the ever-increasing tide of evil swamping the world's crime fighters. And if he still cared enough to drive it.

Today he had something more immediate weighing on his heart.

Despite the hard-won wisdom of experience, and against all the odds, once again he seemed to have arrived at that fateful crossroads with a woman. He realised now that, at some level, recognition of that knowledge had been in his bones from the instant he'd set eyes on her.

The other time he'd reached this point he hadn't had a second's hesitation. He'd plunged in and swept Ariana off her feet without a bare moment's consideration for anything beyond the glossy surface. No objective thought as to whether their hearts and minds could engage and find solace in each other.

Was he in danger of making the same mistake *twice*? His gut clenched as the realisation of what was truly bothering him articulated itself in his thoughts. With lovely Pia, the passion was vibrant, as was all the pleasure, the excitement and laughter. But what of the deeper bonds lovers needed if they were to endure?

Trust should be there, surely. Affection beyond lust. Respect.

He visualised her face the day of their conversation in the café. How she'd mocked him. The possible seriousness of those things she'd said to tease him had gained a sudden traction since he'd discovered she was an artist. She didn't want to be pinned down. Was that the key to her reserve?

Last night he could have sworn her tears had been sincere in her response to the fracture of his life. Yet still she chose not to reveal her own story. Maybe he was making too much of it. Maybe she truly hadn't been affected by what by all accounts most people would find a terrifying experience.

Or was it simply that she needed time?

He had an urgent sense of his own time running out. He'd postponed his return to work but he couldn't indefinitely. Soon he'd have to take up the grim load again. His interlude would be over. He understood enough about love to know that once he left, no promises made, no commitment achieved, the sweet, exhilarating momentum would be lost.

Instinctively he comprehended that last night had been crucial, a turning point between them in some way, yet nothing had been established. The crushing thought crept up on him that perhaps nothing ever would and she'd slip through his fingers.

What then?

He braced his shoulders and faced the relentless sea. Well, then he'd go back to doing what he'd done for five years. Surviving. Filling the emptiness.

CHAPTER THIRTEEN

HALLELUIA. She could paint.

In the days that followed Pia worked on her landscape, and planned out the beginnings of several others in various carefully selected parts of the town. In the absence of an art supply shop in Positano, forced to replenish her materials, she was faced with a dilemma. Nothing but the urgency of needing to capitalise on her power while it was bubbling up inside her could have forced her into it, but she swallowed her anxiety and braved the Blue Ribbon again, quietly catching the bus into Sorrento.

She was hardly relaxed on the journey, but the view from the bus wasn't nearly as confronting as it had been from the car, especially from the side away from the cliff edge.

In subsequent days she became a frequent visitor to the Villa Silvestri. At her tentative request, Enzio agreed to allow her to draw him, and seemed greatly delighted when she showed him the result. After that, it was easy to persuade him to sit for her for a little while every day to be painted.

She didn't expect to finish the portrait in her remaining time in Italy, of course, but she had plenty of good drawings of her subject to draw from, and some well-lit photos. She could finish the work in Sydney. A souvenir.

Since she visited so often, she was almost always invited to share their evening meal.

'We have been talking,' Enzio announced one sunlit

morning on the Silvestri balcony. Valentino was stretched out on a lounger, his long bronzed legs crossed at the ankles as he perused the newspaper. Occasionally he read out amusing snatches or made sardonic comments about the progress of the investigation into the missing Monet from the Cairo museum. 'We are thinking it is your turn. Tonight we are hoping *you* will cook the dinner for *us*.'

'Who, *me*? Are you sure? Two such splendid cooks as your-selves?'

'No, no. There is *one* splendid cook here. And one who is a little...*cosi, cosi.*' He waggled his hand modestly.

'I wouldn't know what to cook for you guys,' she protested. 'I'm no good at risotto, and after that ravioli sauce the other evening I wouldn't dare try to compete.'

Valentino roused himself from his newspaper and said gravely, 'I believe we are in the mood for a Thai stir-fry. Isn't that what you were hoping for, Nonno?'

'*Sì,*' the old man said excitedly. 'A Thai stir-fry is the one thing I am wishing for.'

Pia laughed uproariously at the very notion, but willingly shopped for the ingredients and whipped up her special as part of the evening meal.

When the food was before him Enzio tasted his modest serv-ing gingerly, then persevered, picking his way through it with extreme caution, his face puckered in polite agony. Valentino tucked into his without hesitation, to Pia's intense relief, his eyes brimming with laughter with every glance at the old man's pain.

The delights of Enzio occupied only one piece of her pre-cious, precious time. The best was Valentino, her friend, her playmate, her collaborator by day, her lover by night.

Sometimes he would text her. *I want you.*

Come to me, she'd reply.

Up and down the moonlit steps they slipped to each other's

beds, until her feet knew every dip and rough spot between her gate and Valentino's.

Every magic night she waited, enthralled, for her lover's key to turn in the lock, then he'd stride in as quiet and sure-footed as a big cat, slide under the covers and take her in his arms, the night-scented air on his skin, desire pulsing in his hard body. Sometimes he smelled of the sea and she guessed he'd been out in his boat, though to where he never would say.

Every night held new adventures in excitement, with Valentino virile and thrilling in the fierce heat of passion, yet tender, and always, always concerned for her pleasure.

A couple of times Valentino called her to him, and she flew down the stairs, tingling with anticipation, to where he awaited her in his moonlit courtyard, ready to spirit her into the villa and up the stairs to his bed. Somehow at first light she managed to wrench herself from his arms and run home through the dewy dawn.

'Do you think he knows?' she whispered to Valentino one passion-soaked midnight, when he was resting beside her in his bed, the embers of desire still aglow in his slumberous eyes.

'Sure he knows.'

'Then why must we be so secret?'

A smile crept into his eyes. 'If he knows officially, I will be forced to marry you.'

'Heaven forbid.' They both laughed, but avoided each other's eyes.

Valentino was keen to coax Pia into his boat. At first reluctant, she relaxed when she experienced how skilled and capable he was at manoeuvring the craft, and learned to enjoy the lazy afternoon hours fishing or sailing around the cliffs.

Valentino showed her secret grottoes the tourists never saw, with fantastic stalagmites, and mysterious underwater light that turned the limestone walls impossible glowing shades from turquoise to emerald.

Love held Pia in a state of rapturous suspension. She took

hundreds of photos, but, conscious of her treasured days slipping by, *dreading* the goodbye, she was burning Valentino's beauty into her memory.

She wanted to savour every heart-stopping instant of her lover. Handsome and fit in his old beach clothes, laughing, his teeth a flash of white against his tan. Barbecuing a fish on a little fire he'd built for their lunch on a remote pebbled beach. Sporting with her in the waters of a tiny cove kinder than the one where she'd taken her plunge into the deep.

There was the day he dropped anchor in a hidden inlet, protected from the view of passing vessels by a massive outcrop of rock.

'I am insatiable for you,' he said quietly when they'd finished every crumb of their picnic of prosciutto, panini and mozzarella washed down with wine. 'It will kill me to leave you.'

A blade stabbed her heart and she knew then with certainty that he would leave and she would be destroyed. 'Then don't.'

'Truly?' He kissed her, then rocked her slowly and passionately in his arms to the music of the gulls and the gently lapping waves. But just for an instant there'd been that searching expression in his eyes, doubt, perhaps even remorse, and she knew the day of his departure was closing in.

Wary of spoiling the precious time left, she kept quiet about her search for the cocktail dress for Lola's forthcoming party. Luckily, Positano abounded in boutiques. She found a dreamy, silky, floaty dress with shoestring straps that didn't break her meagre budget, and hung it with her other things in the wardrobe.

Valentino had remained so tight-lipped about her visit to Capri she began to wonder if he'd forgotten. Then on the night before she was due to go, in a moment of respite from passion, he said, 'What time does the boat collect you?' He was leaning on his elbow, tracing the line of her body with his finger.

She tensed, then kissed the inside of his forearm. 'Noon.'

He drawled, 'I gather from that pretty dress I see poking out from that cupboard door you're still set on going?'

'Yep. And I gather from that frown you're still dead set against it.'

'Certamente.'

'But you understand my reasons. I'm not disregarding your experience there. But at the same time I have absolute confidence in Lauren. If I had anything to fear she would never have—'

'Sì, sì. I understand you *think* you must do it for your cousin's sake. But I can't accept it is necessary.' His eyes held hers, fierce and implacable. 'You are forcing me into something that goes against every grain of my being.'

She sat up, studying him curiously. 'What?'

He breathed harshly through his nostrils, looking thunderously grim. 'If you must insist on being so reckless, you leave me no choice. I am coming with you.'

She wasn't sure whether to be thrilled or horrified. On the one hand she was quite relieved to have a companion, on the other she couldn't forget the explosive dynamics of his meeting with Lola.

'They might be very surprised,' she said weakly. 'They mightn't have catered for an extra person.'

A tinge of cynical amusement crossed his face. 'Have no fear,' he said sardonically. 'I will try not to embarrass you. I will behave with the courtesy the occasion demands.'

She bowed her head. 'Maybe that's what I'm worried about.'

She dialled the number Lola had given and informed Lola's boatman that Valentino would sail them to Capri. Though the day of the journey sparkled, the trip across the turquoise water was rather tense, with a silent, inscrutable Valentino at the helm. The buzz of energy she sensed emanating from him could have lit the entire coastline.

'If it's only sex, drugs and rock'n roll you're worried about, I'm sure I can cope with them,' she ventured at one point.

'It's more likely to be sex, drugs and money laundering,' he growled.

She shook her head at him.

What did he have to be so nervous about? They were hardly likely to hold her down and pump her full of narcotics, were they? Or push her off a cliff. Or sling her into a moat filled with crocodiles. From what she'd heard, Lola's husband was rarely even there, so she doubted she'd have to worry about him.

Her biggest worry was more likely to be social. The wife-swapping could be uncomfortable, though she'd be damned if she'd agree to swapping Valentino. And what if her clothes weren't good enough? What if the place was thronging with movie stars? Or, worse, royalty and heads of state?

How did one correctly greet a princess? she wondered. Should she curtsey, a revolutionary like her? She wished now she'd read all those trashy magazines in the hairdresser's with greater attention.

When Capri eventually loomed before them, a giant lime-stone rock formation pointing at the sun, she drank it in eagerly, the craggy cliffs, the whitewashed town sprawling down to the marina where the boats were moored. The massive yacht she'd seen in the harbour at Positano was moored a little way out, riding at anchor on the waves, dwarfing other craft. As they passed it by she craned up at its glossy port side in an attempt to see the deck. It was hardly smaller than a cruise ship.

Dominico was there to greet them at the jetty as arranged, then escorted them to the port where a uniformed driver waited.

Pia barely had time to see much of Capri town, beyond an impression of crowded narrow streets, hotels, restaurants and bars crammed with tourists. Both she and Valentino were ushered into a sporty little car with the top down and whisked up a steep, narrow road overhung on one side with shrubberies and bougainvillea, with hairpin curves and views to rival the Blue Ribbon.

Luckily the trip was brief.

They drove through a pretty village with more whitewashed villas, grander and more luxurious than she'd noticed below. Narrow lanes and picturesque alleys flashed by her, and, at every turn, spectacular views of the island and the bay.

Valentino clasped her hand in his and she clung to it.

'This is Anacapri,' the driver informed them. 'Soon we will reach the Villa Fiorello.'

A few minutes beyond the town the road started another steep ascent. The driver turned down a narrow road little more than a ledge along a cliff, then into a gateway in a high fence of white stone. An avenue of cypresses led them to an elegant, spreading villa with arches and an immaculate garden of hedges and velvet lawns and azaleas. A helicopter waited on the roof.

The driver opened her door for her and she stood on the gravelled drive, looking around and realising from what looked like a massive drop at one side that the villa was indeed perched on an outcrop of cliff, its lower levels cunningly engineered to be flush with the cliff face.

Calm. Calm was what was needed, and a strong mind. She was well past her disorder. She could swim, she could sail, and she'd already proven she could fly in more ways than one. She was determined not to make a fool of herself here before Valentino. Still, her heart-rate picked up a bit, as if to remind her she wasn't infallible.

The driver rang the bell and the grand front doors were opened by another employee, this one in the white jacket of the house steward. He took her bag and Valentino's overnighter with a smooth bow and invited them to follow.

They strolled into a vast white room of silver-veined marble, barely furnished apart from a graceful fountain in its centre. The sun's rays from a skylight positioned directly above it turned the fountain's spray crystalline. Pia turned to exclaim to Valentino, but before she'd had time to fully absorb the miraculous beauty of it Lola appeared from a doorway, then hurried across to them, hands outstretched.

'Pia, darling, and Tino. How you have managed to surprise us, but welcome at last.' If her eyes lacked warmth when they fastened on Valentino, her smile was determinedly correct. 'Some of our guests are here already. Giancarlo is with them by the pool. Let me show you to your rooms.'

Amidst many enquiries about their trip, their health and events in Positano, she led them down long broad corridors to a spacious white room with elegant white furniture, long mirrors and a wide low bed. White satin curtains covered an entire wall.

'This room is one of the most highly prized by our guests,' Lola said, beaming. 'Giancarlo wanted *you* to have it, darling, since it is your first time.'

'Oh, and it is *beautiful*,' Pia exclaimed, overwhelmed by such thoughtfulness. 'Heavens, look at the size of this bathroom. We could give a party in here.'

'It wouldn't be the first,' Lola said with a gurgle of laughter. 'Make yourself as comfortable as you please. And now, Valentino...*your* room...'

'Oh.' Pia exchanged a glance with Valentino. 'I think we'd prefer to share, if you don't mind, Lola.'

Lola's lashes flickered but only for an instant. 'Of course, darling. As you wish.' She made a small moue. 'I wondered, of course, but didn't like to enquire. Anyway, lunch is by the pool, just out there and along to your left. Oh, and you might wish to change. Pool things are in here.' She opened the doors of a cunningly inset wardrobe. 'Don't be shy to make use of anything you see here. And anything else you need, just ring. If it's humanly possible, our staff will provide.'

When she was gone Pia plumped on the bed.

'Just *look* at this place. Wow. To be filthy rich. Are you going to stand around glowering and looking furious the whole time we're here?'

'Not the whole time.' He sprawled beside her. 'Not when I'm looking at you.'

'Good.' She gave him a resounding smack on the lips. After a while she got up to inspect the wardrobe.

'Oh, my God.' Her eyes opened wide.

An entire collection of very scanty bikinis, casual clothes, dresses, frocks for formal occasions, shoes, bags and accessories crammed the shelves and hanging space. The labels were an eclectic bunch. Paris, Milano and New York all figured strongly, with Barcelona well represented amongst the shoes. 'Just look at this. Most of these things are in my actual size. Lola is certainly thoughtful.'

Valentino eyed the collection with a frown. 'Are you planning to wear them?'

'I don't know.'

Lola certainly *was* thoughtful. And she had a pretty good eye for estimation. It was kind of her, utterly generous, to want to clothe her guest like a catwalk princess. Pia wondered if all the guests were offered the same facility. What about afterwards? Should she have the clothes steam-cleaned? What was the protocol here?

She looked at her canvas bag, then with a sigh got up and started to unload it. There was nothing wrong with her swimsuit. It had been fine at Bondi last year, it was fine in Positano and it would be fine here. She just hoped Lola wouldn't be offended if she didn't wear her designer clothes.

In fact, in her view the strappy dress with the butterfly print she was wearing was one of her most flattering. And it still looked clean and fresh. Surely it would do for a pool lunch? Did she *have* to swim?

'Does this look all right?' She got up and examined herself in the mirror, then needing more light, strolled across to the curtains and pressed a button in the wall.

Mistake.

Her heart jumped into her mouth and she reeled back. With an exclamation, Valentino sprang up as well.

Through the glass, seemingly at Pia's feet, gaped a thousand-foot drop. Hurriedly she pressed again and the curtains swished smoothly back together. When her lungs started working and her blood stopped booming in her ears, she forced herself to try again.

This time she stood back a little.

Beautiful, she told herself, breathing carefully. The view was beautiful. A sweeping vista of emerald, blues and aquamarine. Craggy cliffs and undulating shoreline. Pretty villas and gardens. Sea and sky, and, across the bay, Vesuvius. Spectacular.

Deliberately she left the curtains wide open. She could get used to this. She could.

Valentino stood beside her and deliberately pressed the button to close them. 'Do you mind, *tesoro*? I find that view very unnerving.'

She could have kissed the man.

The pool party was well under way. Languid people lay on loungers and sipped drinks, or nibbled the canapés circulated by the ubiquitous staff. The pool, in a vast elegant space with a glass ceiling made Pia think of ancient Roman baths. Some couples were entwined in the water, or hanging at the side chatting, while others stood in bright clusters twittering like rare parrots, eating, drinking and glittering with jewels despite their pool togs.

A few faces seemed vaguely familiar, but Pia couldn't say she recognised anyone famous.

Lola undulated up looking voluptuous in a bikini with a see-through wrap, and took them on a leisurely progress around the groups, introducing them.

A balding grey-haired man interrupted his conversation to shake hands and greet Pia kindly. 'Ah. So you are the cousin of our clever Lauren. You are most welcome.'

Lola introduced him as her husband, Giancarlo.

After the delicious food was served, Lola invited her guests to drive down to the town to visit her little gallery.

Valentino was as interested in the gallery as Pia, so they joined the people piling into the several vehicles and were driven into the village. Pia and Valentino were the only guests interested in viewing the works for sale in Capriccio. Most of the people had been before and wanted to stroll around the streets, look at the shops, possibly with a view to buying something, and visit the *gelateria*.

Pia enjoyed walking around looking at the works, discussing them with Lola and Valentino and hearing their different perspectives.

In the photographic section Pia happened upon one of Lauren's pictures, with a hefty price tag. 'Wow. Lauren's work is worth a lot, these days.'

'Yes,' Lola said seriously. 'Yours could be too, if you were to show here.'

Pia looked at her with surprise and some bemusement. 'You're kind, but how can you say that? You've never seen my work.'

'But I have,' Lola exclaimed. 'Two of your pictures were on the Internet from the South Australian Festival. Lauren showed me.' She glanced across at Valentino, who was examining a modern work across the room, and lowered her voice. 'She's told me so much about you. You and she both have the romantic temperament. Like Lauren you are *un artista*. A bohemian. Your art must be your first consideration. You need…' she spread her arms wide '…*space*. In your home, your life, your friends… A lover who has dreams.' She glanced again at Valentino, and Pia followed her gaze. At the same moment Valentino turned his dark head to look at them. His eyes glinted and Pia knew at once he'd heard what Lola said.

Afterwards Pia and Valentino strolled around the small town, waiting for the other guests to rejoin them.

'Lola is impressed with your work,' he commented.

Pia felt a little jar of warning. 'So she says.'

'You don't believe her?'

'I think she was being—polite. I wouldn't dare to judge any-one's work sight unseen.' She smiled at him and linked hands.

'Still, she seems—very knowledgeable,' he persisted. 'She seemed to know a lot about your needs as an artist.'

Pia shrugged. 'But are all artists the same? I know I'm not the same as Lauren, regardless of what Lola says. In no way the same. We don't want the same things.'

He stopped and faced her. 'What do you want?'

'Well, Valentino.' She smiled. 'You.'

She reached and put her arms around his neck. He gazed quizzically at her for a moment, searching her eyes, then he pulled her hard against him and kissed her.

CHAPTER FOURTEEN

DARKNESS fell on Capri. The day trippers had gone home, and Pia wished she and Valentino had gone with them. She felt a terrible yearning ache for Positano, but, after her insistence on coming, she should at least have the decency to stay the night.

There was a lull before dinner when people were resting in their rooms, no doubt changing into exotic designer gowns. Valentino said he was going for a prowl around the gardens. 'Keep the door locked,' he instructed.

Pia luxuriated in the decadent sunken bath for an hour or so, though she didn't open the blind that hung over it. Admitting her small problem with heights was beginning to feel like half the solution.

As usual, she spent most of the time puzzling about Valentino. He was clearly avoiding all mention of the future, so she could only assume he was being careful of her feelings. It would happen suddenly, she guessed, with no warning. He'd be with her one day, then announce his departure and be gone in an hour the next. At least she hoped he'd say goodbye.

Would they write to each other across the world for a while? She wasn't such a romantic as to nourish any illusions about the longevity of that. Relationships rarely survived such a distance.

Even if they stayed together by some miraculous change in Valentino and the world order, if he needed to travel all the time how would it work? She wasn't the travelling kind like

Lauren. In fact, she was beginning to suspect she was the type who needed to put down roots. Choose a spot, stay in it, and learn all the wondrous treasures it contained, like Enzio and his beloved Positano. Although, if it was the only choice offered, wouldn't she follow her lover to the ends of the earth?

She would. Of course, she would. She allowed herself to dream of it for a little while, then mentally slapped herself. Such dreams brought on heartache, and this wasn't the place to dream anyway. There could be a rattlesnake in her bed and she needed to keep her wits about her.

Dinner was slated for eight. Valentino returned from his reconaissance mission and while he showered Pia dried her hair, smudged on a dramatic quantity of eyeshadow and mascara, and darkened her eyebrows.

It was her first opportunity to wear heels since the night of the fireworks, and she slid into them with girlish pleasure. The tan she'd developed in recent days helped.

Her new dress had fine straps and was ruched at the breasts, falling to a hanky hem that floated about her knees. It was in sea shades of sky, turquoise and aqua, her best colours, with a silvery sparkle here and there. She had no priceless bling, just a fine white-gold chain, but she wasn't displeased with the overall effect.

Valentino emerged from the bathroom in the towelling robe, freshly shaven and smelling deliciously masculine. When he caught sight of her he paused, his eyes riveting to her with a hot wolfish gleam that was supremely satisfying.

How she loved to be appreciated. No other man had ever looked at her like that.

'You're *bella*,' he said thickly, surging across the room to manhandle her in the most pleasant and exhilarating way. 'I could eat you alive. Why don't we stay in our room? We can order room service.'

After she'd fought him off so she could retouch her hair, she watched in the mirror with half an eye while he donned his black evening suit. He looked so lean and straight and honourable and stunning he wrung her heart.

Oh, Goddess and all the Muses. Don't let him leave me yet. Just a little longer.

At the appointed hour, with Valentino beside her, Pia followed the music down a flight of stairs and joined the assembled guests in a beautiful room with arched windows overlooking the harbour. A long rectory type table was set brilliantly with flowers, crystal and silver on starched white linen.

'Bellini, signore? Signorina?'

A waiter presented each of them with a flute of prosecco flavoured with a little peach juice.

'Grazie.'

It was delicious, neither too sweet nor too tart.

When it was time to be seated, Giancarlo took the head of the table, Lola the foot. Their hostess sparkled.

The diners attacked their food with gusto. Course after course of heavenly Neapolitan cuisine was washed down sophisticated gullets by rivers of the most divine wine, and the hum of conversation rose to a roar. Pia tried valiantly to keep her end up with the people in their section, but she found them heavy going. Even Valentino seemed much more concerned with listening to other people's conversations than hers.

After the fifth or sixth course he excused himself and explained to Pia he was returning to the room to make a call. Various people were coming and going, changing places to talk to friends, standing on the terrace to smoke, so the length of Valentino's absence wasn't remarkable, but Pia noticed.

She tried texting him surreptitiously, but there was no reply.

She waited ages, beaming and nodding at strangers until her cheeks ached. When would they bring on the dancing girls? When Valentino didn't appear in time for platters of the most superb selection of cheese and fruit, she excused herself and sashayed up the stairs and through the labyrinth of corridors to the room.

He wasn't there.

So where the hell was he?

Beginning to feel aggrieved, Pia took the stairs down to the next level, then realised she must have come down a different set of stairs. The villa was hardly a hotel, but with eighteen en-suite bedrooms, the possibilities of being lost weren't small.

After a frustrating number of twists and turns, the corridors narrowed and she started to feel disoriented.

She could hear kitchen sounds, and realised she must have wandered into the bowels of the villa. She was about to turn and go back when she spotted, along to her right, what appeared to be the business section.

It seemed a likely place for Valentino. Hurrying, she walked past a study, which appeared to be in darkness apart from a slice of light reflected from the corridor. Across the way was a suite of offices. A handy bathroom caught her gaze, and she took the opportunity to avail herself of the facilities.

She was just emerging when something flashed in the corner of her eye and she spun about. She froze.

A huge man was standing with his back to her, typing into the computer in the dark study. He was all in black, from head to toe. She wouldn't necessarily have been so concerned about him if he hadn't been wearing a ski mask.

Fear crushed her lungs in a vice. She stood motionless, unable to breathe. The fear inhabited her entire being, rendered her legs useless and shut down her brain, until from out of nowhere a wild wave of seething hot anger roared through her like adrenaline.

Galvanised, she tiptoed towards him, intending to slam the study door and lock him in. But as she advanced something must have alerted him, because he started to turn around. Quick as blinking, she dashed forward, snatched up a small bust of Tiberius from a plinth in the hall, and whacked him over the head with it.

He must have sensed the blow coming, because he held up his arm and deflected it a little. Even so, he went down like a log.

Darting back, she slammed the door shut. There was no key, so she just stood there holding the door handle with both hands, panting and triumphant, congratulating herself on her victory, gloating on a cloud of exuberant liberation.

She, Pia Renfern—*Pia Renfern!*—had downed a man in a ski mask.

After a minute she noticed no sound issuing from the study, and it occurred to her to wonder how hard she'd hit him. The Emperor Tiberius had a pretty hard head and had caused the demise of more than one miscreant in his time.

That reflection filled her with horror. *What if she'd killed him?*

She put her ear to the door, but couldn't hear a sound except her own thundering heart. After a tense moment, she relaxed her grip on the handle and stood back. When nothing happened she turned the door knob carefully, waited, then pushed the door a little ajar. There was no sound or movement.

She pushed the door wide, then jumped back.

The body had disappeared.

She let out a partial scream and nearly died when she was grabbed from behind and a firm hand covered her mouth.

'Shh. Don't make a sound. It's me. It's only me, *tesoro.* Valentino.'

Her knees went to water.

He closed the study door and locked it from the inside, then switched on a desk lamp and supported her limp progress to an elegant chaise longue along one wall. He was obliged to push aside a pile of newspapers and package wrapping to make room for her.

She started to wail. 'What are you *up* to? Take that thing

off your *head*. You scared the living *daylights* out of me. You frightened me so much…'

He dragged off his balaclava. '*Sacramento*, that thing's hot.' He dropped it on the desk, then dropped down beside her and put his arm around her. 'I know, I know. You weren't supposed to see me in it. I'm desolated to have scared you, *tesoro*, truly I am. But why didn't you stay in the dining room? I told you where I was going.'

'But you didn't go there, did you?' she screeched. 'You came here.' She knew she was stating the obvious, but why couldn't the man make sense?

'Shh, keep your voice down.' He frowned and groaned. 'Oh, *Sacramento*, why did you have to hit me so hard? Were you trying to *kill* me? I have a bump on my head as big as a soccer ball. Just as well I was wearing that mask or I'd be—*kaput*.'

'You deserved it, scaring me like that.' She reached up to smooth down his hair but he winced at her light touch. She pulled her hand back.

'Shh,' he murmured. 'I told you. Keep your voice down. Giancarlo might come back at any minute. Or any of the staff.'

'What are you even *doing* here? I can't *believe* this. I thought you were a burglar. I know you loathe these people but you promised you'd behave. Pia, you said, I'll never embarrass you. You know you said that.'

'Pia. Pia, *tesoro*, shh, shh, calm down now. It's all right.'

'Is it? Is it, Valentino?'

She might have clipped her consonants a little. And the glare she gave him was chilly. But her provocation was strong, even if he did keep touching a spot on his head as if it was causing him pain.

'Look,' she snapped, 'I've been waiting for you for hours at that deadly dinner party. Would you care to explain what you're doing breaking into someone's private study dressed as a burglar? Otherwise I might be forced against my will and my—my personal inclinations to call the police.'

A piercing gleam lit his eyes. 'You'd do that?'

'I think I would. Yes. I'd certainly consider it.'

He smiled to himself. 'My kind of woman.'

She gave him a shove that didn't even make a dent. 'This is no joke, Valentino. I'm deadly serious.'

'I know. And I'm sorry. I'll explain later.' He kissed her cheek, then rose swiftly and went back to the computer.

She knew he was too caught up in his nefarious downloading to pay any attention, but she was so wound up, she couldn't stop talking, twisting her hands, babbling on like the Brisbane River in flood.

'I don't think you can have any idea what it means to me to see a man in a ski mask.'

He glanced up at her, his gaze sharpening. *'Cosa?'*

'I wasn't going to tell you this. I probably need my head tested. You…of all people… A *carabiniere* who's been in the navy chasing pirates and smugglers. Anyway, it sounds miniscule when compared to what you went through with your ex-wife. I honestly don't know how *anyone* could survive something like that. You must be made of pure steel. You'll probably think I'm as weak as water if I—I tell you…'

Her chin started to wobble. Dismay and concern registered on his lean face as emotion took hold and her tears started to fall like rain. He abandoned the computer and surged across to hold her, making little soothing noises in Italian as he had the morning she'd nearly drowned.

He gave her a handful of tissues from Giancarlo's desk and she blew her nose and managed to drag herself together.

Even for him his eyes were curiously bright. 'Tell me. When you're ready. I want to know everything.'

'You see, a few months ago something happened to me that was really—quite scary.' She attempted a smile. 'I walked into the bank one morning, just an ordinary, everyday morning like any other, and these two guys came in behind me. One grabbed me and stuck a gun to my head and threatened to blow my brains out if they didn't hand over money, while the other one ran around terrorising the staff.' She shrugged.

'Oh, no, *tesoro*.' But he didn't make light of it, he continued to gaze down at her, his face grim, his intent dark eyes aglitter. 'What happened?'

'Well, unbeknown to us all, as soon as they walked in one of the tellers had bravely...so, *so* bravely...stood on the alarm button, and in no time the police came roaring up from all directions, sirens blazing. They—the robbers—lost their nerve. The guy holding me threw me on the floor, then they both ran out the back and tried to squeeze themselves through the washroom window. Police were swarming all over the place by then and caught them without much trouble. Everyone shouting... screaming...'

She shuddered, remembering, and he held her tightly against his chest and kissed her hair and stroked her. She could hear his big strong heart beating. Surfacing again after a while, she gave him a watery smile. 'You know, when that first police siren sounded, there was a moment when I believed the guy would do it. I actually felt him tense to pull the trigger. I don't know what changed his mind, we'll never know that, but thank God *something* did.' She dashed some tears away with the back of her hand. 'Anyway, I think that was when it happened.'

He gazed at her, frowning, '*Cosa?* What else happened?'

'Oh, well...'

Could she admit her weakness to him? He looked so intensely concerned, his acute dark gaze so grim, yet tender and encouraging. He'd told her all his stuff. For goodness' sake, maybe he of all people could understand hers.

Her throat swelled and predictably the monsoon started again, like the certified waterworks she was. 'Don't laugh, but I—sort of lost my nerve. After that day I was scared of everything, even going outside the apartment. For a while I was a—a mess.' She attempted another watery grin. 'You'd never believe it to look at me now, would you?'

'Never.' He drew her to him and kissed her face and hair. 'I can hardly believe *you* were ever a mess. Not you. Not a free spirit who flies around the world all by herself.' There was the slightest tremor in his deep, warm voice. He kissed her long and tenderly until she had to come up for air, and somehow they were lying down, crammed together on Giancarlo's chaise longue amongst all the newspapers and rubbish.

'I'm so glad it was you I told,' she confided. She could feel the raw energy throbbing in his lean, lithe body like the power source of the cosmos.

'And I'm glad you did, *amore mia*. You'll never know how glad, what it means to me.'

'Really?' There was a certain promising thickness and warmth in his voice that she recognised. However, something was sticking into her hip, and she had to change position to re-move it before she could fully reciprocate his affections. 'Hang on.'

She shifted the offending article, noticing it was a crumpled parcel. Its brown-paper wrapping had come unstuck and the bubble wrap and layers of cloth inside were all awry.

Noticing the inner layer was a canvas, she unrolled it a little in order to rewrap it. Her eye fell on a narrow swathe of painted water. She opened it further. Lotuses floated on a French pond. She stared incredulously.

'Oh, look. Look at this.'

'Che cosa?'

'Oh, my God,' she screeched. 'I can't believe this. This looks quite amazingly like that Monet that was stolen from the mu-seum in Cairo.'

He sat up, his sensational brows bristling, his brilliant dark eyes agleam with curiosity. 'Give me that.'

He practically snatched the priceless thing from her. After a long hard look, he shoved it back to where it had been. The next thing he was on his feet, shutting down Giancarlo's com-puter. Whipping out his mobile, he dialled, held the phone to his ear, murmured a couple of words, then slipped it into a pocket and grabbed her arm.

'*Andiamo,*' he said briskly. 'We're leaving.'

'What?'

He let out an exasperated breath. 'Pia, the *carabiniere* are about to arrive here and I don't want to stay. Do you want us to be in the newspapers?'

'How do you know?'

'I've just been talking to them.'

'But…but what about my things? My gear, my…my painting bag?'

'You can get them all tomorrow. Come on. *Pronto* now.'

'Tomorrow? How? You don't think I'm coming *back* here, do you?' She said this as he was hustling her onto a window ledge, leaping out himself, then holding out his arms to her.

'Jump, Pia. *Pronto.*'

She stared down. They were at the side of the house, not the cliff side, thank the Lord, in fact only a few feet from the ground, eight or ten perhaps as the crow flew, but it was an abyss.

'Pia,' he said firmly. 'Jump.'

Heaven knows how, but she did it. Straight into his arms, and for the second time that night flattened him to the ground.

'Woof,' he sort of said as the wind was knocked out of him. After a few seconds she scrambled off him, and he heaved himself up, panting. Then he made her run. An alarm started to blast from somewhere inside the house, and there was a worse sound.

Far worse.

Dogs, great savage dogs with slavering jaws, and nothing could have inspired her more to keep running with Valentino, and let him bundle her through a hedge, drag her through garden beds and hoist her up on top of a stone wall.

Somehow he shinned up there himself, paused for less than an instant and landed lightly down the other side.

'Andiamo,' he said again, holding out his arms.

It was child's play this time, especially as the hounds from hell accompanied by bellowing men had burst into the front yard. Luckily, there was a car waiting, or was it a car? The vehicle had a strange shape, a roof but no windows.

Fortunately for her nerves the thing started, and Valentino was able to swing it out into the narrow road and speed them down through Anacapri to the port. On the way through Anacapri they passed a whole brigade of silent, ominous-looking dark vehicles with white roofs and red stripes along their sides heading towards the Villa Fiorello.

After that she kept her eyes closed until he was hustling her along the jetty and into the boat.

'Now,' he said, settling back once they'd cast off and were heading across the bay towards Positano. 'There are some things I probably need to tell you.'

CHAPTER FIFTEEN

'I should think there are,' Pia said drily, though in truth she felt thoroughly invigorated and curiously uplifted by the recent adventure. 'I must say though, I wouldn't mind trying a little breaking and entering myself once in a while. It's energising, isn't it? We could set up a partnership.'

Valentino gave her a shocked, incredulous glance. 'Wipe that out of your mind,' he growled. 'You will be doing no breaking and entering. Pia Renfern has broken all the laws she is going to.'

'I haven't broken any yet.'

'No?' His eyes glinted. 'Not even a little traffic infringement? You must indeed be an upright citizen.'

She smiled and leaned against him. In truth, he felt so satisfyingly solid. 'I'm sorry I whacked you on the head. It all seems so surreal I can't believe it all happened. What were you up to in Giancarlo's study? Honestly?'

He didn't speak, then after a moment he cut the engine. In the sudden silence, broken only by the sounds of the sea, his deep voice appealed to her ear like the music of the spheres. 'I—haven't yet told you everything about my work. The truth is…'

Something in his tone gave her deep misgivings. She sat up and stared at him.

'We have known for some time about the Fiorello couple. They have some dubious connections, but it's not so easy to find evidence. It takes time to correlate searches through tax records. It was good to see there was some hard evidence there for the *carabinieri* to find. I have you to thank for that.'

She homed in on the crucial word. 'We? Who's we?'

He barely hesitated. 'Have you heard of Interpol?'

'*Interpol?* What? You're kidding, aren't you?'

He sighed. 'No.'

She blinked several times, trying to take it in. 'So you—you work for Interpol?' The bottom was falling out of her world, yet she felt this insane desire to laugh. 'So I've been sleeping with an Interpol agent.' She chuckled.

'No, you've been sleeping with Valentino Silvestri.'

The gentle correction was lost on her as she continued, 'I cracked an *Interpol* agent over the head.' Another chuckle escaped her, then he joined in and their laughter rang out across the dark water.

Still smiling, though his shadowy eyes looked almost sad in the starlight, Valentino said, 'It was pretty funny, I guess. But you know, *tesoro…*'

A fearful realisation sank through her then and she felt pain, such a deep, despairing pain. She said, 'I suppose you'll be leaving now.'

He turned to look at her. 'I find I'm at a strange crossroads. Either I go one way, or another. I stay with Interpol, or I resign. I remain on the shelf, or I decide to leap off.'

She held her breath. 'Where would you leap?'

'Into the arms of someone I love.'

'Oh.' As realisation began at last to sink in she had the thrilling sensation that the moon and stars were inside her and lighting her up like phosphorescence.

Hardly daring to hope, her heart thundering like an avalanche, she breathed, 'Are you saying…?'

'*Sì.* It is you. I am meaning you, Pia.' His dark eyes were warm and sincere. 'I'm so in love with you, I can't think of

leaving you without a pain in my heart. Would you consider...
marrying a simple Neapolitano?'

Her heart swelled until smiles burst from her like sunbeams.
'I would consider it.' She put her arms around him. 'My darling Valentino. My dearest love. Indeed I would.'

* * * * *

SEPTEMBER 2011
HARDBACK TITLES

ROMANCE

The Kanellis Scandal	Michelle Reid
Monarch of the Sands	Sharon Kendrick
One Night in the Orient	Robyn Donald
His Poor Little Rich Girl	Melanie Milburne
The Sultan's Choice	Abby Green
The Return of the Stranger	Kate Walker
Girl in the Bedouin Tent	Annie West
Once Touched, Never Forgotten	Natasha Tate
Nice Girls Finish Last	Natalie Anderson
The Italian Next Door...	Anna Cleary
From Daredevil to Devoted Daddy	Barbara McMahon
Little Cowgirl Needs a Mum	Patricia Thayer
To Wed a Rancher	Myrna Mackenzie
Once Upon a Time in Tarrula	Jennie Adams
The Secret Princess	Jessica Hart
Blind Date Rivals	Nina Harrington
Cort Mason – Dr Delectable	Carol Marinelli
Survival Guide to Dating Your Boss	Fiona McArthur

HISTORICAL

The Lady Gambles	Carole Mortimer
Lady Rosabella's Ruse	Ann Lethbridge
The Viscount's Scandalous Return	Anne Ashley
The Viking's Touch	Joanna Fulford

MEDICAL ROMANCE™

Return of the Maverick	Sue MacKay
It Started with a Pregnancy	Scarlet Wilson
Italian Doctor, No Strings Attached	Kate Hardy
Miracle Times Two	Josie Metcalfe

**SEPTEMBER 2011
LARGE PRINT TITLES**

ROMANCE

Too Proud to be Bought	Sharon Kendrick
A Dark Sicilian Secret	Jane Porter
Prince of Scandal	Annie West
The Beautiful Widow	Helen Brooks
Rancher's Twins: Mum Needed	Barbara Hannay
The Baby Project	Susan Meier
Second Chance Baby	Susan Meier
Her Moment in the Spotlight	Nina Harrington

HISTORICAL

More Than a Mistress	Ann Lethbridge
The Return of Lord Conistone	Lucy Ashford
Sir Ashley's Mettlesome Match	Mary Nichols
The Conqueror's Lady	Terri Brisbin

MEDICAL ROMANCE™

Summer Seaside Wedding	Abigail Gordon
Reunited: A Miracle Marriage	Judy Campbell
The Man with the Locked Away Heart	Melanie Milburne
Socialite...or Nurse in a Million?	Molly Evans
St Piran's: The Brooding Heart Surgeon	Alison Roberts
Playboy Doctor to Doting Dad	Sue MacKay

Mills & Boon® Hard Back
October 2011

ROMANCE

The Most Coveted Prize	Penny Jordan
The Costarella Conquest	Emma Darcy
The Night that Changed Everything	Anne McAllister
Craving the Forbidden	India Grey
The Lost Wife	Maggie Cox
Heiress Behind the Headlines	Caitlin Crews
Weight of the Crown	Christina Hollis
Innocent in the Ivory Tower	Lucy Ellis
Flirting With Intent	Kelly Hunter
A Moment on the Lips	Kate Hardy
Her Italian Soldier	Rebecca Winters
The Lonesome Rancher	Patricia Thayer
Nikki and the Lone Wolf	Marion Lennox
Mardie and the City Surgeon	Marion Lennox
Bridesmaid Says, 'I Do!'	Barbara Hannay
The Princess Test	Shirley Jump
Breaking Her No-Dates Rule	Emily Forbes
Waking Up With Dr Off-Limits	Amy Andrews

HISTORICAL

The Lady Forfeits	Carole Mortimer
Valiant Soldier, Beautiful Enemy	Diane Gaston
Winning the War Hero's Heart	Mary Nichols
Hostage Bride	Anne Herries

MEDICAL ROMANCE™

Tempted by Dr Daisy	Caroline Anderson
The Fiancée He Can't Forget	Caroline Anderson
A Cotswold Christmas Bride	Joanna Neil
All She Wants For Christmas	Annie Claydon

Mills & Boon® Large Print
October 2011

ROMANCE

Passion and the Prince	Penny Jordan
For Duty's Sake	Lucy Monroe
Alessandro's Prize	Helen Bianchin
Mr and Mischief	Kate Hewitt
Her Desert Prince	Rebecca Winters
The Boss's Surprise Son	Teresa Carpenter
Ordinary Girl in a Tiara	Jessica Hart
Tempted by Trouble	Liz Fielding

HISTORICAL

Secret Life of a Scandalous Debutante	Bronwyn Scott
One Illicit Night	Sophia James
The Governess and the Sheikh	Marguerite Kaye
Pirate's Daughter, Rebel Wife	June Francis

MEDICAL ROMANCE™

Taming Dr Tempest	Meredith Webber
The Doctor and the Debutante	Anne Fraser
The Honourable Maverick	Alison Roberts
The Unsung Hero	Alison Roberts
St Piran's: The Fireman and Nurse Loveday	Kate Hardy
From Brooding Boss to Adoring Dad	Dianne Drake